HOLLYWOOD

CONNOR

COYNE

LETHE
PRESS

"With evocative and true-to-life prose, this story gave me the visceral experience of being young—of that magical time in life when your friends are your family and every future is possible."

LEILA SALES
author of *This Song Will Save Your Life*

"Like a dream that leaves you wanting more, *Hollywood* pulls you along an atmospheric journey of self-discovery and human connection. Evocative and moving."

BONNIE JO STUFFLEBEAM
author of *Where You Linger & Other Stories*

"This book beautifully captures the complexity of hope through use of metaphor and enjoyable descriptive storytelling."

INDEPENDENT BOOK REVIEW

"A poignant portrait of young people making art and mischief, magic and memories, on Chicago's North Side, the kind of mystical place where even a mile-long shark is not the strangest experience on tap. *Hollywood* is about found family, and about the brief, precious season in which it flourishes, and it made my heart ache."

WILLIAM SHUNN
author of *Inclination* and *The Accidental Terrorist*

ONE AUGUST AFTERNOON, IN THE midst of the hottest years ever recorded, with the nation crashing through wars, the stock market climbing like Icarus toward the sun, and the City funneling its poor people inland as it closed and demolished the last of the projects, Ophelia got off the Red Line elevated train at the Thorndale stop, squinted in the sunlight, and kicked her foot against the platform to free a stone from her sandal.

"Home at last?" she asked herself.

She certainly hoped so. There was so much here, and all of it everywhere: dozens of dark smears from murdered bubble-gum on each sidewalk square, hundreds of quartz-bright sidewalk squares lassoing each block, and thousands of glowing, sweltering blocks throughout the City with its millions of people.

To the west, between the tracks and Broadway, Ophelia made out a video store, a laundromat, and an internet café, all noisy with activity at four in the afternoon. To the east, between the tracks and the lake, she saw a canyon of tenement apartments—mostly brick, fronted with stoic windows, several stories high—going out for three blocks before the real high rises rose from the beach, blue and white and glass and concrete, almost unimaginably tall. Their heights arrowed sunlight back toward Ophelia, hitting her from all sides. And here, too, she saw people coming and going in the glow of late summer.

"Please," she said. "Let this be my home."

But who was going to answer her? Not the smartly dressed Black men talking in low voices, laughing softly, leaning out over the tracks to look for the next train. Not the old Polish woman in the headscarf murmuring her rosary to herself. Not the train attendant patrolling the platform. Or the sun, the steel high-rises, the brick tenements, the video store, or the laundromat.

Since nobody would answer Ophelia, she descended the stairs, passed through the station, and went out into the City.

ᑐᑐᑐᑐᑐ

FIVE MINUTES LATER, OPHELIA STOOD in the lobby of her new apartment building, buzzing for the super to come down and give her the keys. The building stood near the corner of Kenmore and Ardmore, just one block from Sheridan Road and the lake. At eight stories high, it was the tallest of its neighbors, though still dwarfed by the towers just a block away. A white stucco lobby. Moll carpet. Plastic plants standing in shell-shaped alcoves cut into the wall. Nothing fancy, but with a breeze coursing down the hall from an open fire escape, Ophelia's new home felt luxurious.

The super arrived and eyed her new tenant suspiciously. Ophelia wasn't tall, but she was so skinny, especially about her face, that it created an illusion of height. When she looked in the mirror, her prominent cheekbones reminded her sometimes of a skull and sometimes of a praying mantis. Ophelia was white, pale even, with fine brown hair that wisped gently about her shoulders. She generally considered herself a fairly okay-looking person, whatever her other defects might be. Still, she knew wrinkles and exhaustion were about the corners of her eyes. Anyone could see this. Everyone noticed. She was only in her early 20s but seldom got carded for alcohol.

The super frowned but must have decided Ophelia was harmless because the woman hit the button in the wall, and the elevator dinged in reply. The super pulled open the accordion gate, and as they rose through the building, Ophelia watched each floor sinking out of view. She tried to ignore the stench of stale piss. They got off at the seventh door. The woman fumbled with the keys, swearing under her breath in some Slavic language, and opened the door to Ophelia's apartment.

She'd seen Tasia's pictures, but they didn't do justice to the place. The hallway opened into a long white living room with a white carpet and a bay window looking out to the east. Slivers of blue water peeked in from between the lakeside towers. An arch to the left led into a slender kitchen, all Formica and old appliances, while another hall exited the back of the living room, passing the first bedroom and the bathroom and ending at a second bedroom with plenty of closets and built-in shelves along the way. Ophelia spotted a cockroach crawling across the stovetop and another in the back bedroom. Still, there was something so happy and fierce about the light and the skylike linearity of the lake that hope welled up in her chest anyway. This was fine. No, glorious! She'd deal with the roaches later. Maybe after Tasia arrived.

As Ophelia carried out her inspection, the super stood in the living room with her hands on her hips, waiting, but there wasn't much else for Ophelia to do: everything had already been settled.

Several months ago, she had told Tasia that she was going to off herself before the end of summer if she didn't get out of Rockville. "Let's move to the City," Tasia had said. "Get jobs. Get a cheap apartment. Hit the beach. Hit the good stuff." The joke came up several times before the friends realized that they took the idea seriously. Even though Tasia'd gotten her Associates from the community college, she seemed stuck in dead-end cashier's jobs and was dying of boredom. Rockville was killing her slowly.

And killing me quickly, Ophelia thought. She'd only been half kidding about surviving the summer. So, before she knew it, the two were creating profiles on Monster. com, Googling neighborhoods, and emailing old friends from high school who had moved to the City. Tasia drove out one weekend, picked up some job applications, toured the apartment on Kenmore, and signed the lease. She'd gotten in on a special promo: no security deposit required. Ophelia had faxed her signature. They were in.

But if Tasia had set the whole thing up, she also needed another week to tie up the last loose ends at Spencer's Gifts. "My manager got caught stealing inventory," she'd said. "They want to promote me. I haven't broken the news to them yet." So, Tasia stayed behind while Ophelia went ahead with her sleeping bag and a backpack full of cleaning supplies. To get the new place ready. To make it homey.

Ophelia thought back to the 4th of July weekend when she'd lain in Tasia's bed with Tasia on top of her and Rockville's fireworks bursting out the windows. The taste of shandy on Tasia's lips and her sturdy weight pressed down. How all the wretchedness and sorrow of all those years had collapsed that one drunken night. So ... were they friends now? Roommates? Lovers? Friends-with-benefits? With all the planning for their big move, this was one thing they hadn't discussed. Ophelia wasn't sure if it complicated things or simplified them.

"Okay?" asked the super.

"Thanks," said Ophelia. "It's wonderful."

"Okay."

As if on cue, a dull thudding sound—four-to-the-floor with the bass bass bass—started thrumming down from the apartment overhead. The eighth-floor penthouse.

"Uhhhhh," groaned the super. "They never stop."

She let herself out, leaving Ophelia with the music.

〰〰〰〰〰

IT TOOK OPHELIA ONLY A short time to unpack. She chose the second bedroom, near the back. It didn't have a view of the lake, but it got more sun, and she could see the long sweep of high-rises following the shore and rising toward their downtown crescendo. Since she didn't have a dresser or bed, Ophelia stacked her clothes in neat piles along the wall, unrolled her sleeping bag in the middle of the floor, and crushed a cockroach with her shoe before it could scurry for cover. Then, with the music still thudding overhead, she shouldered her backpack and left the building.

Ophelia found a supermarket just past the Thorndale stop on the other side of the tracks and spent the next half-hour in a reverie, pushing a shopping cart up and down each aisle and wondering what the next month held in store. I could apply to be a cashier here, she thought. I could apply to be a teller at that bank across the street. I wonder if I could apply to work for the El trains. I'll need to make money somewhere! She didn't worry a whole lot about what she did or didn't need to buy. She had a crisp hundred in her wallet—a parting gift from her grandpa and some keychain pepper spray—but this was just the first of many shopping trips. Right now, she just needed to make it through the next week. She bought some Bisquick, some eggs, and milk. Instant coffee. Bananas and apples. Bread and peanut butter. A dollar box of cookies. A six-pack of cheap beer. Paper plates and plastic forks. A tall can of Raid. A small pillow. It ate up half of her money, but it was enough. She was halfway home before realizing she had nothing to cook the pancakes in or boil water for coffee. I can go back tomorrow, she thought. The peanut butter and beer will keep me going for tonight.

When Ophelia made it back, the sun was lower in the sky, and shadows covered the streets below. The thudding upstairs continued. She set her keys and phone on the counter, massaged her sore arms, and noticed that she'd missed a call from Tasia.

"Tasia?" she said when her friend answered.

Tasia gasped. "I didn't think you'd call back so quick!" she said.

"Why wouldn't I call back quick? I was carrying groceries. What's up?"

"I'm bursting! I'm bursting! I can't lie! I can't come to the City with you!"

"What?"

"I was going to turn down the manager job, O, but that was before they made the offer. I didn't know it came with such a huge raise. They're gonna pay me twelve an hour. That's, like, twice what I make now! No way I will get a job in the City that pays that much. And you know how expensive it is there ... have you seen the gas prices yet?! We didn't think this through, O. I can't move now. It would be crazy. I mean, it would be fucking stupid. I mean, I'm gonna get fucking health care!"

"Slow down, Taze. We have been planning this for months!"

"I know, I know, I'm so sorry, it was my mistake too. It was just a dream, you know? It was a silly dream. A summer thing."

"But our names are on the lease!"

"No security deposit, remember? So, we're out that first month, but I'll make that up in like a month. Maybe two. Point is, I'll make it up quick! You could get out. It was my fuckup. I signed the lease. We just walk away. Hey,

I'm the manager here now. I can hire you. Think how fun that'll be. We can work at the mall together. Lunch at the food court. You know you love them burritos!"

Ophelia's heart was sinking. It was already in the basement laundry room, and maybe it wouldn't settle until it reached the bottom of the lake.

"I don't know, Taze," she said. "I was ... I was really excited about this. For us. I ... went shopping."

"Oh, shit. How much money do you spend on us, O? It's okay, I can pay you back. Now I'm, like, rolling in money! Compared to what I have been. You'll come back to Rockville, right?"

Ophelia looked helplessly out the window. A seagull sailed down the street, caught between cool breezes from the lake and the warmer currents wafting off the brick buildings.

"I don't know, Taze. I don't know anything right now. You shocked me. I mean, you surprised me." She took another long pause. "I have to think about it."

"I understand. I'm sooo sorry to just drop this. But I'd be crazy not to, you know?"

"I know. I get it."

"Call me when you make up your mind. I'd love to hook you up."

Would you love to hook up?! Ophelia cried out in her brain. What does this mean? What did that mean? What does anything mean?

"I will," she said. "I'll call you soon."

"Hey, nothing else, we're paid up through the end of September. Take a vacation in the City before you come back!"

〜〜〜〜〜

IT WASN'T ANYTHING, OPHELIA THOUGHT. It couldn't have been much. She was drunk, and I guess I was desperate. Am desperate.

Ophelia went into the kitchen and took another look at the food she had bought. She probably had enough money left over for a pot and a pan, but she wasn't sure that would leave enough for public transit, and if she wanted to get a job, she'd need some train fare. She decided that she could boil water for coffee in a pan, leaving her enough to take the train downtown for a week. That's ridiculous, she thought. Who lives like this? If I go back home, I've got a sure thing at the mall. I can go back to Grandpa and Grandma's. Maybe save up. Maybe try again in a year. Or two. Maybe Tasia and I get a thing going ... if she wasn't just drunk. If she really meant it. A car on the street below started honking. The honking continued, and Ophelia realized the driver was waiting for someone to come out of another apartment. She was drunk. She didn't mean it. There's no way I can stay here, and there's nothing for me to go back to there, either.

Between the thudding bass and the car honking, Ophelia was starting to get a headache. She wanted to bang against the ceiling with a broom but didn't have one. She opened a beer with the bathroom towel bar, using the trick her brother had taught her. She shotgunned the beer, then had a second and a third, and then she was halfway done, so she went to the bathroom for a pee and drank the rest of the beers on the toilet. By then, she was getting dizzy, but at least drunkenness was a temporary relief. The honking had finally stopped, but the bass thudded on. Ophelia went into her bedroom and shut the door, thinking it might muffle the sound, but it didn't. An elevated train of alcohol slammed into her skull. She giggled sadly and reeled. Ophelia knew she was just as drunk as she'd been when she'd tumbled into bed with Tasia, but she was all alone this time. The walls and windows swirled around her, the bile danced in her stomach, and her ears popped like fireworks.

"Shut up!" Ophelia said and fell asleep.

〰〰〰〰〰

CASCADES OF SHIMMERING LIGHT. WATERFALLS of light. Blue light, purple light, iridescent, black light, effervescent, bubbling through her dreams, like the time she had been among the fireworks with Tasia and then again, the time she had seen the fireworks with her mom and her grandma and her grandpa when she was little, on a sloping green lawn back in Rockville. A drench of honeysuckle. Dragonflies hovering like miniature helicopters. It doesn't have to be a bad life back there, she spoke to herself, hovering above the earth like a still-winged angel. There is beauty and people you love. You could have some of the things you want. You could be happy sometimes.

Ophelia woke in gray light. An hour had passed or two or more. The music upstairs was softer now, a gentler track, a more leisurely rhythm. The bedroom had stopped its carousel, but the headache hadn't. I haven't left, it seemed to say. I'm just getting comfortable. Soon, Ophelia knew, the ache in her temples would spread across her skull. Would squeeze with fingers of pain. She got up, opened the window, and leaned out to get a look to the west. The sun hadn't set yet. Not quite. But the buildings were tall enough that their shadows stretched long into the east.

Ophelia fished around in her backpack until she found a sandwich bag with some Advil. Popped them and drank deeply from the tap. Wiped her brow. Thought about taking a shower, but she didn't have towels. Something else I forgot, she thought. Fucking idiot. For a minute, she strolled from room to room in the darkening apartment, and then she found herself out in the hall, pushing the button, getting on the elevator, getting off on the first floor, and walking out into the evening.

If the neighborhood had been busy when she'd arrived, it was swarming now. Dozens of sedans squeezed up the one-way streets, each looking for the single spot nobody had noticed, "goddammits" ringing against the fire hydrants that stood proudly upon their yellow-painted curb strips.

Ophelia found herself back up on Thorndale, walking under the El tracks, back to the supermarket, buying herself two tallboys of Steel Reserve. No need to save my money if I'm just heading home anyway, she thought. Am I heading home? I guess so. I'm spending all my money. Then, cradling the precious paper bag against her stomach as if it were an infant, she made her way back under the tracks. She didn't return to the apartment this time but kept on past Kenmore and Sheridan. She kept finding herself. Every moment, Ophelia looked at herself in light of the surroundings she had audaciously tried to claim. This spectacular city. Its density. Its possibility. Who did I think I was? Whatever I thought, I'm obviously the town idiot here.

Now, she found herself standing on the edge of a desolate, shell-crusted beach. The signs called it:

HOLLYWOOD BEACH

She'd come to see the sunset, but Ophelia couldn't spot it anywhere. Then she noticed the towers' long shadows reaching ahead of her and over the water and remembered the obvious: The lake is to the east. She opened one of her tallboys and took a deep drink. Fuck it. She continued onto the beach.

It was larger than Ophelia had expected. Because she'd only caught a few small glimpses between the big buildings, she assumed that each block had its own tiny strip of sand pressed between the heights. Instead, she discovered a broad sandy stretch running south for many blocks, banked against high-rises, and vanishing into the blue water. A few teenagers and younger kids scrambled over an outcropping of rocks that rose from the shallows, marking the northerly end of the beach. Out in the water, a lifeguard sat in a clunky rowboat, yelling through a megaphone at a handful of swimmers who didn't stay within a stone's throw of the shore. He won't have to worry about me, Ophelia thought. I didn't even pack a swimsuit. Why bother? She couldn't swim. She took another gulp, wondering if the City's cops were as lax about public alcohol as they were in Rockville. It doesn't matter, she thought. They can ticket me if they like. I'll be gone soon. She strained further, wondering if she could see the farther shore of the lake, but there was no way. This lake was huge. One of the hugest in the world. She might as well have been standing at the edge of the ocean.

Ophelia made her way south, sipping as she went, the shadows lengthening over the purpling water, ambered chandeliers winking on in the high-rises, and a small crowd of men in speedos and designer sunglasses clustered in front of her. They were just now starting to pack up for the night, beers and volleyballs, striped blankets and umbrellas, and Ophelia realized that she was the only woman here and that none of the men seemed to be a decade younger or older than her. Is this a gay beach? she wondered. There were a couple gay bars in Rockville, but she hadn't ever heard of a gay beach before. Somewhere behind the buildings, the sun had finally gone down, and the fire of orange overhead became blue bruises. The wind off the water picked up with a rush, scattering sand rippling umbrellas, and the last of the beachgoers turned their backs on the lake, laughing as they went.

Ophelia had reached the end. A rocky break wall rose from the water, with grassy hillocks and small groves of trees replacing the sand, and a few concrete piers thrust out, dividing the choppy waves. The nearest of the piers extended farther than the rest with a steel turret at the end, topped by a winking red beacon. By now, the beach was almost entirely empty. The lifeguard had come ashore and lashed his rowboat to a concrete post.

Ophelia walked onto the pier, sidled around the beacon, and sat with her back against it, her legs hanging out over the lake. She couldn't see the bottom, but the waves were large, forbidding. Ophelia didn't like deep water, and she figured if she fell in here, she was as good as dead. But the cables and concrete reassured her, and she tilted her head back for a long, deep drink.

What happened? Ophelia asked herself. What went wrong? Besides Tasia's totally predictable change of heart when she realized she'd be able to make more money doing something easy and natural. She'd have to uproot everything. That's not a problem for me. There's nothing back there. I was ready to leave. I knew I wouldn't change my mind.

And that reflection went halfway to answering her question: It wasn't a matter of what had gone wrong. Rather, nothing ever seemed to go right, and Ophelia had stupidly imagined that this time might be different. An unpleasant thought. Unpleasant thoughts deserved to be murdered with big gulps. She tilted her head back and took in more Steel Reserve, its buzzing, hoppy bite sizzling and burning deliciously down her throat. She swallowed, crumpled the can, and hurled it into the water.

Ophelia wasn't sure at what point things had been the most fucked. She'd run away a few times as a kid, but back then, she was just aping her parents, who were always running away themselves, leaving her and her brother alone for hours, sometimes days in a row, with peanut butter in the pantry and beer in the fridge. When she was nine, she ran away from her dad again, but he was gone too, and her grandparents got the cops involved. Two weeks, a CPS intervention, and an ankle monitor later, Ophelia was living with her grandparents, and things should have gotten better from there. But the drama never stopped. Another unpleasant thought, so Ophelia cracked open the second tallboy. I have to go back for more, her thoughts slurred. I'll try sipping this time.

She tried to memorize the water before her the way it was now. Mostly dark but not yet entirely stripped of daylight. The windows behind her fired silver bullets of illumination into the choppy waves. Ophelia saw a couple of distant sailboats, and these seemed to be making for the shore. She took a sip. There had been the part where the city was falling apart, and they closed all the high schools except one. There had been her hookup with Andre, the pains that followed, and a supposedly secret trip to a clinic that ended when she discovered her grandparents parked by the curb, glaring at her through the haze of exhaust. Their doors were still open, but the warmth was all gone, so Ophelia had dropped out of school and moved in with some friends up on Olympia Street.

There was plenty of the next few years that she didn't remember. Plenty that she did remember but tried not to think about. Plenty of adrenaline from those days. Alcohol and dopamine were purchased dose-by-dose through barter and charm, and once by pulling hair, screaming, and ripping her friend's back to shreds.

That was one friendship that had died forever and that certainly deserved more than a sip. Ophelia took a long, long pull. The water looked darker now.

But she had seen, some nights, on the couch or on the floor, where her life was heading, in the footsteps of her dad and her brother. Their roads smelled like mildew and mothballs. Felt haunted like a storm sleeping in her bones, threatening, bringing the ache. So, one day, she enrolled in school again and got her GED. She got a job at a party store and worked at Cherry On Top in the summer. She moved back in with her grandparents, and if the old warmth had left for good, so had the anger. Ophelia's life wasn't happy, but it wasn't miserable. She even got her old bedroom back. She started to reconnect with old friends. The ones she'd left behind. Brit and Lacey and Tasha and Tasia. And that summer, Tasia had said they should move to the City together, and Ophelia had thought, she had dared to believe: I don't know. Maybe? Maybe this time?

But even if she could stay now, she wasn't sure why she should.

The City seemed less magical now that Ophelia knew she wouldn't share it with Tasia.

She lifted the can for another sip, but from the corner of her eye, she saw something moving in the water. She lowered the can. Is it close? she wondered. Is it far out? It was a dark shape but surrounded by luminosity. By many points of scattered, amber light. She climbed shakily to her feet to get a better look.

The thing was enormous and far off, but it was too dark by now for Ophelia to gauge the distance precisely. The water receded, revealing sand and stones just beneath the waves. Out toward the horizon, Ophelia made out an oval shape, dark, with a sail upon its back. For a moment, Ophelia wondered if it could have been a submarine, impossible as that seemed. Then, she realized it was much larger than a submarine and wondered if it could have been a freighter, even though the shape was all wrong.

The shape moved and answered her question for her. The shape surfaced more fully, revealing itself as more of a bullet shape or a torpedo, and it opened its eyes and its mouth. Its eyes glowed like fire and lava, its teeth glinted like sharpened spears, and Ophelia saw the snout, gills, dorsal fin, and tail shimmering and glittering. The truth was obvious, and there was no other way to interpret it: it was a tremendous shark.

The shark seemed to grin where it rested, miles out into the lake, its bright eyes fixed in position as it studied the twinkling City and Ophelia standing paralyzed beneath the winking beacon, on the pier, on the beach.

The creature opened its mouth wide, wider, closed, swiveled a little, and submerged.

Its dorsal fin sank last of all.

Ophelia continued to stand, shivering in the wind. Did that just happen? she wondered. Did I just see that? *A shark in the lake? As large as a mountain?* Did I just –

And then the wake came. Massive waves, six-, eight-, ten-foot high, raged in from where the shark had submerged and roared against the pier. Ophelia screamed, dropped her beer, and ran back toward the shore as fast as she could, her legs soaked, her hair wild, the waves snarling behind her. Once she reached land, she kept running: up the grass and up the beach and between the buildings and across the streets and into the building on Kenmore, where she took the smelly elevator back up to the seventh floor and ran into her curtainless room and knelt down on the floor and wrapped the sleeping bag around her head and tried to shut her eyes against the vision of the monster. But she could still see it, sitting there, staring at the City, staring at her, hiding its intentions, giant and silent and all alone.

~~~~~

OPHELIA COULD HAVE STAYED THERE all night.

She could have lain there buried, quiet, and safe until the sun came to banish the memory of what she'd seen looming on the horizon. Then she could call her grandma to buy her a ticket, ride the El back downtown, and catch a train back to Rockville. She shouldn't have tried to fly so high. The universe had given her all of the hints along the way, and she'd ignored them, so now it was sending her more than hints. Now, it answered her with myths.

But the sound got to Ophelia long before the daylight did.

At first, she thought that she felt her headache returning, and she knelt more deeply in the sleeping bag and squeezed her eyes shut. The pulsing didn't stop. It was all music. The thrumming upstairs continued. Now, two beats clashed against each other, slightly out of sync, every so often coalescing for a moment before gliding apart again. One beat, closer, came from the space directly over Ophelia's head. The other, louder but more distant, must have been from the main room of the upstairs apartment.

Ophelia tried to ignore the sound, but it was a primal, foundation-shaking crunch. Something not designed to be beautiful or ugly but simply unignorable. Even if she could have shut it from her mind, her bones would keep singing along. Ophelia finally jumped up, threw the sleeping bag onto the floor, and screamed, "Shut up! Shut up! Shut the fuck up!"

The sound continued.

Ophelia stomped into the kitchen—there seemed to be a third beat originating from upstairs now—and checked the time on the oven. 11:15.

She left her apartment, turned into the stairwell—cinder blocks and steel railings—and hauled herself up to the eighth floor, where she confronted the door of apartment 801, throbbing with bass and laughter. She banged on the door. She banged again. Nobody answered but she was pissed now—*I'll do them like we do in Rockville!*—and she turned the knob and stepped inside.

〰〰〰〰〰

IT WAS DARK ON THE other side of the door. Ophelia heard muffled voices and laughter nearby but couldn't see anyone. Her eyes started to adjust. A curtain of purple light glowed right in front of her. Something bright and blurry. She blinked, focused on the image, and recognized it as Doc from *Snow White and the Seven Dwarfs*, inches from her face. He was either whistling in surprise or wearing his "o" face, looking solicitously at the laughing princess, frozen mid-clap though the beat hadn't stopped. Snow White rippled. So did the dwarves. Ophelia was looking at a projection upon a dark bedsheet hung in the tiny foyer over the archway leading to the living room. She pushed through the curtain.

The room beyond was almost as dark as the foyer had been. A purple rope light sinewed around the base of the room, following the line of the walls and throwing shadows upward. Two boxy computer monitors arrayed beneath the windows broadcast greenish streams of hieroglyphics Ophelia recognized from *The Matrix*. And out those humble windows, the contours of the towers on Sheridan Road rose forty stories and higher, many of their windows amber with more sedate evenings. This was all the light that filled the room.

Between Ophelia and these meager illuminations moved a dozen or so shadows. A couple of them danced. A couple others nodded heads. Most simply talked loudly over Orbital's gyrations booming from a bank of impressive speakers. Despite the darkness, Ophelia sensed this was a thoroughly Caucasian crowd.

"Hey!" shouted Ophelia.

"Hey!" shouted a nearby shadow.

"I live downstairs. This music is too loud!"

"What?"

"I said *the fucking music is too fucking loud*!"

"Oh, shit! That sucks!"

Ophelia studied the speaker. A face floated in the space above a baggy sweater and skirt. The face looked as smooth as a blemishless pear. Ophelia figured this was a "she." It sounded like a woman's voice ... she thought.

"I don't know these people," the speaker went on. "But we'll see if we can find someone to turn it down."

The speaker turned to another shadow.

"Do you know who we ask?" she asked.

"Beats me," the other shadow said. "I'm from downstairs. But Stan lives here."

"Who's Stan?"

"Stan's got the ponytail!"

"Follow me."

Ophelia felt fingers tighten about her hand and pull her deeper into the room, amidst the many shadows, over to the computers. A gold light shone from the narrow kitchen – the floor plan of this apartment evidently mirrored Ophelia's exactly—where a tall, lanky man, all knees and elbows, nursed a Solo cup of who-knows-what.

"You're Stan, right?" asked the woman.

"Yup!" said Stan.

"Your neighbor here says it's too loud."

"Sorry," said Stan. "Ferin says we've got to have it loud."

"Well, I just think maybe it's kind of rude now that it's night to have the music this loud," said the woman.

"Yeeeeeah," said Stan.

"I just moved in—" began Ophelia, copper tracing her tongue.

"Yeah, yeah, you're right. Not everyone wants to stay up all night, eh?"

And with a twist of the knob, the beat faded subtly, still loud but no longer threatening to break the building into ruin.

"So, you just moved in, eh?" asked Stan.

"Yeah."

"Glad you made your way up! We hoped more people would come out tonight. Help yourself to some food and booze."

"Where's the booze ... and food?" Ophelia answered without thinking. When you've grown up poor, you take what's offered.

"Right this way!" Stan said, passing through another curtain.

Orange light and violin music filled the narrow kitchen. Ophelia saw a small round table and two mismatched chairs that had obviously been scavenged from an alley, some recently cleaned and disinfected countertops—she breathed a trace of bleach on the air but still saw a couple of roaches fried on the range—and a fridge, and another half-dozen people. In the light, Ophelia got a better look at Stan and her shadowfriend.

In addition to the knees and elbows, Stan was clean-shaven with an angular face, long brown hair in a neat ponytail, and a delighted, slightly drunken smile. The shadowfriend wasn't smiling, but she had a pleasant face and seemed in a good mood. She had short, blonde-brown hair in a pageboy cut, canny dark eyes, and was already moving in on a scratched baking bowl full of bright orange popcorn.

"Food is popcorn and chips," said Stan. "Booze is Mike's, and Killian's, and Guinness's, and some rum and cokes, too."

"You're Michiganders like me?" Ophelia asked.

"Yeah?" said Stan.

"I knew ..." said Ophelia, angling in at the Castillo's. "We always apostrophize shit."

"Fuckity fuck, you're right."

Ophelia poured herself a cup of rum and topped it off with a bit of Coke. She drank deeply.

"So, who are all y'all?" she asked.

"I'm Stan," said Stan. He pointed to each partier in turn. "That's Matt and Colm," an awkward whiteboy with plenty of stubble talking with another short whiteboy with fire-engine red hair. "That's Ferin and Olivia who planned this thing. Ferin's my roommate, but Olivia lives on the South Side." He gestured to a third awkward whiteboy, though this one seemed almost angry, scribbling upon a white index card with angular jags and a young white woman, tall with gray-streaked hair, muttering in his ear. Behind them, a white poster board hung on the walls with RULES written in jagged Sharpie followed by a long list of notes. The "rules" included "Don't break character" and "Nobody leaves until the murder is solved." "And that's Ashley," said Stan, pointing to a very slight, sapling-thin white woman with long, straight, black hair. She was looking out the window at the high rises. She seemed distracted like she was trying to decide what to say next.

"Who are you? Who's your friend?" said Stan, mugging over his solo cup, looking at Ophelia and her shadowfriend.

"Oh, we," said the shadowfriend. "We don't know each other. I'm Clyde. I'm with Violentina. She told me to come on up."

"Oh, yeah, Violentina," said Stan. "I met her on the elevator the other day. Well, help yourselves, eh!"

He upended his solo cup and returned to his precious computers.

Everything hurts crossed Ophelia's brain, but nothing hurt. Her body. She felt like she was advertising to herself. Don't I mean, 'everything's confusing?' Her thoughts were slurried but not slurry enough. She knew the rum wouldn't really hit for another fifteen minutes. Why's it take so damn long? She looked out the window. The ranks of high-rises captivated her again. Nothing like this in Rockville, she thought. Nothing like this in Michigan, really. But between them, she saw the purple line of the lake. The lake where the shark lives.

"I used to paint all the time," someone said.

Ophelia looked up, startled. It was the beautiful sapling woman, and her hair was a curtain like a waterfall interrupted, like a moon on a pool, like the wind in the chimes, like —

"I don't anymore," the woman said. "I kind of gave up on it after college. Not gave up. Just. Other things came up, you know?"

What was your name? Ophelia scratched her brain. Someone just told me your name!

"I'm Ashley," said the woman.

"Ophelia." She hoped she didn't sound drunk now. She wondered if they should shake hands now. She held out her hand, and Ashley shook it awkwardly. "I saw a shark out on the lake," Ophelia said. "It was way out there." She started with horror. "It was gigantic. Miles long. I wondered if it was going to destroy this city."

Ashley followed Ophelia's gesture to look out the window again. Now, she focused on the line of the lake.

"People see strange things out there," she said. "At twilight. At midnight. Visions and demons and northern lights. But all I ever see is the light. It's so bright here at night you can't make out any stars. Not that I want to go home."

"You're not from here?"

"Nope."

"Me neither. I get that."

"Most of us here come from somewhere else. For me, it was a way to get away. My friend's aunt was a serial killer."

"I understand—"

"Hey Ashley," came a voice. A man's voice, deep but as smooth as honey. The man was clean-shaven and openly drunk, but his smile was gentle.

"Brendan? You're here?!" Ashley answered, surprised, delighted, thrilled even?

"I just got in."

He enveloped her in a hug. He was almost two feet taller than her.

"But I need to ask Olivia about her projections," the man said when he finally released her.

"I can tell you about them," said Ashley, "because she told me all about them. I came early. I helped set them up."

And Ashley led the man through the curtain and back into the living room.

Matt and Colm were having some sort of an argument about the Catholic Church. Ferin finished writing on his index card and shook out his left wrist. The side of his palm was covered with faded ink. The woman with the gray-streaked hair—Olivia—laughed and took a big drink. Everyone seemed full of conversation and each other, except Clyde. Ophelia looked at Clyde. Clyde looked back with a slightly ironic smile and shrugged happily.

Ophelia went through the curtain back into the living room.

The lights hit her again. There were too many of them. The violet stars that sang and stabbed. The green glyphs scrolling the screens. The inverted glow of the animated projection was soft on the backside of the hung bed sheet. Above all, those hundreds of apartment windows, rectangular against the lines of the streets, the lines of the sky, the line of the lake at last. I can't really be this drunk already, Ophelia thought, and she was right. Her tolerance had been hard won, and it was honest and predictable. No yeah, this experience was alcohol accented, but the lights were acting on their own. Yeah, no, not alone. These lights were acting in response to the coalescing shapes and shadows in the purple-blue room where she stood. The shadows were humans, and these humans had white skin and freckles and hair on their legs and armpits, and they laughed un-self-consciously and talked about whatever was on their minds. Looking between the lights, the shapes, the lakes, Ophelia could have sworn she saw Rockville fireworks bursting out over the horizon and, maybe, just maybe, in between, a behemoth shark upon the water. But those fireworks! Those tiger lilies! Those lilacs! That phlox! Jesus Christ, if she didn't imagine herself standing under fireworks, but now, instead of a grassy field in the middle of downtown Rockville, it was out on a pier in the City with the bronze-burnished crown of the planetarium glinting behind her. Instead of holding Tasia's hand, she was holding Ashley's. A thought—*insane!*—landed upon her: What if I stayed. I mean, what if I just stayed. What if I didn't go back? What if I just stayed, for me? And she shoved that lovely, terrifying thought back toward the night and dreams because it felt precious, even if it looked absurd. She didn't want to let herself mock it.

"Hey, I think you're new here," came a friendly voice.

"Hey, I think you're new here!" it came again, and Ophelia realized that the voice was talking to her. That the words had repeated because she hadn't answered.

"I'm sorry," she said. "I didn't see you when you talked to me."

She was talking to the ginger. He was standing with his red shirt and a red cup in his hand.

"So, do you know Ferin and Stan?" he asked.

Ophelia shook her head. "I'm from downstairs," she said. "I came up to bitch because the music was too loud."

"I'm glad you did. I couldn't hear my own voice until a few minutes ago. But now I can actually talk," and he chuckled. He awkwardly transferred a newspaper from his left armpit to his right, his right hand with his red cup, and held out his other hand to shake. People seem like they are all their parts added together and not the whole of them. It's like it's only possible to be a bunch of parts, not a whole person. Ophelia shook his hand. It wasn't sweaty, firm, but not rough.

"I'm Matt," he said.

"So ... do you know Stan and ... is it, Ferin?"

"Yeah! Ferin and me, and a lot of us, went to the university on the South Side. Now he's throwing these art parties, and I guess he has people helping him out with it."

"Stan and ... Olivia?" She was learning the names.

"Stan used to join us for these festivals we'd have down there. But I don't think I've ever met Olivia before ...."

"What about Ashley?"

"Ashley went to college with us, too. You go to college here?"

"No, I ...." Ophelia thought better of it and cut her explanation short. "And are you from the City, originally?"

"No," said Matt. "Milwaukee."

"Matt!" came a voice from the kitchen. Colm was sticking his head out from behind the curtain. "We have, um, something to, um, resolve."

"Something involving the Latin Mass?"

"No," said grinning Colm. "Something involving tequila."

"Excuse me," said Matt, and he passed through the curtain and vanished. As he did, Olivia decided to leave. *I don't know anyone.* She edged her way out, her hand in her hair, her face austere except for a single frustrated line between her brows. When she got to the foyer, she paused. Something felt incomplete. Unspoken. She touched the projector, burned her fingers on the lens, and yanked her hand back. She put her hand into her mouth and cooled her burning fingers against her tongue. She angrily unplugged the machine. Snow White and the dwarves blinked into darkness. Ophelia sighed and returned through the curtain.

On the other side, she found Clyde talking with a svelte woman, elegant yet unpoised, in a black dress, black boots, black tights, black nail polish, eyeshadow, and eyeliner, and a black fan.

"... called me a goth," this woman said, scorn in her voice. "That's not who I am. I just like the twilight is all, and Rozz Williams."

Clyde subtly rolled her eyes. The woman didn't notice, but Ophelia did. Clyde noticed Ophelia noticing, and Clyde smiled for the second time that night. She looked down at the carpet, slipping her hands into the pockets of her pants, which were overalls, "aw shucks"-style. Ophelia laughed.

Now Ferin emerged from the kitchen, shuffling his pack of index cards, followed by Colm and Matt, and Ashley and Brendan had returned, and everyone else was now gathered in the living room. Ferin walked about, distributing the cards with a nervous smile.

"Oh, hi," he said, pressing a card into Ophelia's hand.

"Hey," she said. "I'm living right beneath you."

"The music!" Ferin said. "I'm so sorry it was so loud. That apartment's been empty for like two months. We honestly didn't think we were bothering anybody."

"It's better now. It got me out of that apartment. I saw a giant shark on the lake. I was hiding out. Now I don't know. But what's this?"

"A shark on the lake?" Ferin said. "That's a mystery. Don't sleep on that. No, we gotta check that out. I mean, what if it wants to kill us or speak to us? But, um, you know these cards, they're mysteries too." He tapped the card. "The card gives your identity, your secret, and your goal. You have to talk to who you can talk to and see what mystery you can solve."

Ophelia squinted at her card.

Name: Maggie Duncan

Identity: You are a madame at a brothel in Harrison, MI, in the 1870s–1880s.

Secret: You murdered a lumberjack before you married your husband.

You helped your husband bury murdered lumberjacks in the forest.

Goal: You want to steal enough money to move to a big city and live large.

"Damn," said Ophelia.

She doused the last of her rum coke and chucked the empty cup toward the windows. It landed with a rattle behind the computer monitors. This was the final expression of her anger at her noisy neighbors, and they didn't trouble her anymore. In fact, she crossed over to the speakers and turned the music up again, though just a little. These seemed like decent people, like some of her friends back home, but possibly, just possibly, a tiny bit less fucked up. And Ashley was enchanting, and Matt was decent, and Ophelia was starting to suspect that Clyde might be a haruspex.

She approached the nearest shadow she hadn't spoken with and tapped them on the shoulder.

The shadow turned around.

"Hey," said Ophelia. "I'm Maggie. Who are you?"

〉〉〉〉〉〉

AND SO, ANOTHER TWO HOURS passed.

Some of the guests were way into the mystery, to

the point of putting on Canuck accents and affecting lumberjack appetites. They pressed Ophelia about Maggie's secret while trying not to reveal their own. Other guests went along with the premise more or less; they were having fun, but it had more to do with music, booze, and friendship than unburied 19th-century ghosts. And a few of the guests—Matt—just couldn't get into the thing, try as they might. They became the wallflowers, hanging in the shadows, peering out windows, chuckling nervously, and waiting for the conversation to turn.

Ophelia flew among all three crowds. It was all conversation and nourishment to her, and it didn't matter whether she represented herself as the girl downstairs or as a 19th-century madame as long as she didn't have to be "that washed-up kid from Rockville." She talked to everybody and talked to them as they wished. She got to know them all a little. Gray Arsenault came in drag, hoping to empty his bank account and open a corner store on the South Side. Pearl Newsome, Olivia's sister, a doctor and journalist pushing thirty and worried about "all these kids getting into trouble." Chris Caroline, who'd just gotten laid off by McKinsey after never working a day for them—"but the severance was nice"—and she didn't deny sleeping with Stan, but she did deny that she was attracted to him. And others, too: Ophelia talked to Olivia and Ferin and Angel Wilde (Ferin's girlfriend, who put up with these Happenings with the patience of a saint), and Brendan (who had just come in from Marquette and bragged that he was even taller than Stan) and even Violentina, the Gothiest not-a-Goth Ophelia had ever met. Everyone seemed fun, tedious, naive, sweet, tender, and decent, and Ophelia started to love them a little. It felt strange to feel love for people she had only spoken to for a few minutes, but she couldn't doubt the affection. It was their clueless kindness that convinced her. She strongly felt that if she got blackout drunk, she could trust these people not to do any sketchy shit while she was passed out on the couch. She wasn't sure if this was a healthy feeling or not.

Ultimately, the Mystery devolved into a game of Werewolves, which was just like Mafia, except instead of the mobster offing innocents one at a time, it was a bunch of peasants trying to survive the lycanthropes marauding through their village. Ferin had planned the mystery, but Stan eased its transition into Werewolves. Ferin was the man with the plan, but Stan was a better improviser.

Finally, after the second round, during which Werewolf Ophelia had succeeded in murdering every—*yes, every*—villager in Transylvania, the party started to wind down; ordinary lights came on overhead, the weird party lights went off, and she found herself in a conversation with Eliza Steinham, who was very much Colm's girlfriend.

"So, this has to have been a totally crazy night for you, huh?" said Eliza.

"What do you mean?" asked Ophelia.

"I mean, you've just gotten into town, like, today, and now you hear this horrible loud music that just wakes you up, and you come up and hello! You're mobbed with all these people."

"It's been a long day."

Eliza smiled. Ophelia liked Eliza. She was an East

Coast woman and wasn't politely deferential like all of these Michiganders and Wisconsinites. She wasn't rude either. She just got to the point a lot faster. She had short black hair and a frank "I know as much as you do" face, and Ophelia found that refreshing. Back in Rockville, in the houses where Ophelia had squatted sometimes, in the houses where her friends, or "friends," lay on sleeping bags or mattresses with tattered blankets after the heat got turned off, and it was February outside, she got asked these awful questions: "Hey, O, how we gonna eat tonight?"

Maybe the answer was scrounging and returning pop bottles, or maybe the answer was stealing from the party store or something worse. But regardless of what the answer was, nobody wanted to talk about it, so Ophelia would lie: "I'll ask Mr. Marcus if he can give us some money for some pizzas."

Eliza had had a glowing life, Ophelia knew. Someone never once said to her: "Hey Eliza, how are we gonna eat tonight?"

And Eliza, for all her clarity and knowing, for all her honest and blessed frankness, wouldn't have known how to answer that question. But Ophelia felt that, in her place, Eliza would not have lied. She felt that Eliza would have died before lying. So, it was complicated then because Ophelia loved Eliza for her purity and clarity, and she also resented Eliza for her purity and clarity. And Ophelia suspected Eliza knew this and didn't hold it against her. Ophelia wouldn't have said that Eliza was her favorite person at the party ("Ashley and her smooth calves, shaped like an ankh, or that symbol thingy at the beginning of the music sheets, on the top, the sweet notes, the ones girls' sing,"). Still, she thought Eliza was the best person at the party.

And, oh, the rum was singing now.

"Hey," said Ophelia. "Is, um, Ashley, like with Brendan?"

"We've got to go," said Colm, stepping awkwardly into the conversation. "If we're gonna take the Red Line, we won't get home until after three."

"What time is it?" asked Eliza.

"Almost two."

"Jesus, I've got to work tomorrow too," said Eliza. Turning back to Ophelia: "The short answer is, I don't know. I don't think so. But I don't think she's available either. For, um, females—"

"No," said Ophelia, "I didn't mean."

"I didn't think you did or didn't."

And once Eliza had left with Colm, Ophelia realized that she was almost the last person left at the party. Ferin and Angel were doing dishes in the kitchen. Stan was talking to Chris about staying the night, and she seemed receptive. Violentina had ditched Clyde, who stood there, hapless, hands in the pockets of her overalls. Aw shucks.

But Ophelia felt restless.

"You tired?" Ophelia asked.

"Not particularly," said Clyde.

"You want to go for a walk?"

"Sure."

〈〈〈〈〈

THEY SHARED THE SILENCE ON the elevator ride down to the lobby, watching through the metal grate as each floor floated up and away. Ophelia wondered if she should say something about the smell of pee and laugh that the pisser had definitely been a dude, but she was afraid any joke would have sounded forced, so she kept quiet. She wondered if Clyde had finished high school on time, gone to college, and got a good job right away. She wondered about Clyde's age. Clyde looked like she could have been a year or two older than Ophelia, but looks can be deceiving. She wondered if Clyde had had her teeth fixed and if Clyde would notice Ophelia's jagged teeth. The elevator arrived at the lobby. Clyde swung the gate open and held it for Ophelia.

"I can almost hear what I'm thinking again!" said Clyde.

Her teeth don't look perfect, Ophelia thought with relief.

Out of the street, the City would never forget its own density. There were simply too many people, and even at two in the morning, some of them were out, cruising for parking spots, talking in low voices, or knocking back something sour out of brown paper bags. The streetlights beamed down like the rays of a UFO, but "Listen!" said Clyde, and Ophelia listened.

She couldn't hear anything besides the distant rush of traffic.

"What is it?" she asked.

"Cicadas," said Clyde. "Even in the middle of all this, you can hear them."

Ophelia strained and caught, elusive, quiet, the creak of a few lonely creatures.

They started walking. Ophelia didn't know where they were going. Their path took them under the El tracks and across Broadway. The neighborhood beyond was less towering but full of six-flat tenements and large stucco houses, fancy style. Ophelia stopped worrying about what to say and enjoyed the motion of their bodies through the alternating beams of light and shadow, occasionally spiced by dew on sprinklered grass or the stink of a garbage sack sitting at the mouth of an alley. Eventually, the silence must have worn on Clyde because she started talking and picked up speed:

"I've just been there a month. That building. It smells awful and amazing. Like piss or Bosnian cooking, you know? I finished out college and needed a place to stay. I mean, I was crashing on Violentina's couch, and she was boss about it, but who wants to live in a living room? I needed my own place. Did you get the lease without the deposit? I heard about that, and I couldn't pass it up. It was just too good. I don't even care if there are roaches."

So she was at college, thought Ophelia.

"So, you know her?" she asked. "Violentina?"

"Her name's Sarah, but don't tell her I told you that."

Ophelia smiled. "I won't. So, you mean you don't know any of those others. At the party?"

"I've seen some of them around. Stan. Ferin. Stan kind of hooked up with Violent. He's a bit of a slut. I mean, so is she. So, it's cool. But no, not really. Everyone else I just met tonight. I think they're mostly up from the South Side. But I feel like I know them now. I'm usually right if I'm really careful about my first impression. It's a gift. And a curse."

"I don't think I know them," said Ophelia. "Eliza, maybe, a little. But I feel like I know you more than any of the others. And I really don't know you at all."

"You don't?" said Clyde. "I mean, don't you?"

I don't know you, but I want to know you, Ophelia thought. I know there's a lot to know about you. A lot to you. *To you.*

After another block, they came upon another business strip. This one was narrower than Broadway, cuter, more yuppieish, with tanning salons, antique shops, coffee stops, and tiny taverns tucked into its narrow brick storefronts. A few lonely cars slowly trawled the night, but the sidewalks had emptied now that the bars were closed.

"So, you went to college here," asked Ophelia. "Are you from here?"

"From the suburbs. Tinley Park, if you need to know."

"That doesn't mean much to me, sorry."

"Hey, it doesn't mean much to me, either. I had to get out. That place was choking me out."

"I know how you feel. My home kinda choked me out, too …."

"I got a job at the hospital downtown. The one just off the Mile, by the lake. It's, like, one of the tallest hospitals in the world. I work on the eighteenth floor. I know that doesn't sound like much, but when I eat lunch, I can look out over all those big buildings, and it makes up a bit for the shit they pay me."

Maybe Clyde gets me a bit more than those others did.

"What do you do?" Ophelia asked. "Are you, like, a nurse?"

Clyde coughed out a laugh.

"I wish!" she said. "Didn't you hear? I just finished college. Not certified. No way. No, I majored in Sociology. How fucking stupid was that?"

"Is your job, like, a sociology job?"

Are you going to visit houses like my grandparents' and talk to kids like I did back then?

"Nah, nah, I wish, though; I mean, I get paid more than a social worker, just about. Nah, I just needed a job. I gotta eat. I had to get off Violent's couch, you know? I'm just a file clerk. You go in there, you see all those medical charts lined up nice, and they're not a mess. That's thanks to me, you know?"

"I do!" said Ophelia, with a small laugh. A small laugh seemed appropriate. Clyde seemed so confident. "So, if you don't like your job, why don't you get a better one?"

"What do you mean?"

"I mean, you graduated. You could do social work, right? Get a job as a social worker? Instead of being a file clerk?"

"It's not that simple."

They passed in front of a closed bar. A small crowd stood in front of the dark door, smoking. Ophelia and Clyde stepped through the smoke and breathed it in.

"I gave up smoking," said Clyde. "Still like the smell, though."

"Me too," said Ophelia. "I mean, exactly me too. It brings back memories. Good memories."

"To me, cigarettes smell like waking up at midnight and working all night long. With boss music, too."

They walked on, and Ophelia meditated on what she shared with Clyde, the firmness of Clyde, her solidity, and the solidity of the black parking lots, and the shopping carts scattered akimbo between the corrals and the supermarket—there seemed to be many places to buy groceries in this city—and the clickety-clack of the elevated tracks that sounded so different from the mournful train wails back in Rockville. Active and companionable, not so desolate and cold.

"... I'll probably be staying here," Clyde was saying. "... one of the biggest cities ..." "... I could live in another big city, but not a small city. Not a small town, you know. Or the countryside. Nah, I'm definitely a city girl."

Ophelia nodded to acknowledge.

"This one is so big," Clyde said. "It's like a hundred cities packed into one. And wherever you go, you get to see something completely different. There are neighborhoods here, you don't even hear English. You'll hear Spanish, hear Polish, hear, like, Vietnamese or Chinese or Korean. Once, this one neighborhood, I don't think I heard anything but French. Blew my fucking mind! Where even does that happen? In the U.S.A.? I mean, I didn't even think that was possible. Quebec, I guess. But, I mean, it blew my mind!"

Clyde was on a tear. Ophelia watched her face as they walked. She studied every detail. Far from the unadorned oval she had caught in the dimness of the party, Clyde wore a mole in the middle of her otherwise blemishless left cheek, and it moved up and down whenever she opened her mouth as if agreeing with her, nodding along. Clyde's eyes were brown and textured and expressive. She seemed to have energy to spare and no reluctance to share her thoughts, whatever they were. Ophelia suspected that Clyde had been often disdained or dismissed by others, but she seemed not to care. She wouldn't quell her voice on behalf of some ignorant motherfuckers. Nah, fuck that.

"And besides!" Clyde was gesturing now, excitedly, with spirit. "Just this neighborhood, Edgewater Beach, even if you never cross Foster or Devon or Ashland, all the things you can do right here! You've got the shops, you've got the theaters, the galleries, the museums! You've got all the food—I mean supermarkets and farmers markets and restaurants—and the El and the beach and the parks and—"

"The beach!" Ophelia couldn't keep the elation from her voice. "Can we go to the beach?"

"Sure!" burst Clyde. "It's almost on our way back. Let's check it out!"

They left the dainty business strip and turned back toward the lake.

As houses floated by—the streets seemed to have emptied, finally—Clyde caught her breath, thought a moment, and said: "You know, the coolest thing in my life was my parents' motorhome. Isn't that just sad?"

"What do you mean?"

"My dad retired. They kind of laid him off, but he got this big payout—big for them, I mean—and my parents decided to buy a motorhome. Thing gets the worst mileage. I'm sure the insurance is hell, too. They don't go many places with it. Sometimes, nowhere. But they did it up with Christmas lights and got all this camping gear for it. They park it in their driveway, and once or twice, when I was home from college during the summer, I'd go and sleep out there. Lie down on those stiff cushions and look out the windows at the stars, or try to."

As they walked, Clyde seemed to be groping for words with her mouth and her mind. Ophelia watched her.

"When I'm here in the City, when I'm in Edgewater, there are a thousand amazing things I can see. But when I'm back with my parents in Tinley Park, that motorhome is the coolest thing anywhere."

They walked two more blocks in silence. Two more blocks without traffic. The wind sang a grace note of attrition. It pulled at Ophelia's hems. Just a little. Saying, "Hey there." Her palms sweated. Her palms twitched. She felt a desire—the blood in her face—to take Clyde's hand in hers, but how would I explain that? And why would I do that? And slowly, the lake rose into view.

"What about you?" Clyde suddenly asked, soft-voiced.

"What about me?" Ophelia echoed.

"Well, I've been talking about myself all night. Probably bored the hell out of you. So, who are you? Besides Ophelia. Because I do know your name."

"I finished high school and got a job back in Rockville. It's not a very big place. It's got a lot of trouble. A lot of drama. I wanted to make it here. But my roommate bowed out, and I don't have a job. So, I guess I'll head out tomorrow."

"Head out where?"

"Head back there. Back home."

They had almost reached the beach. The beach was right there. Just a few steps away, the sand lay like sugar before the onrushing waves. But the waves were still so far back that Ophelia couldn't hear them.

"You moved out here without a job?" asked Clyde.

"I was hoping for the best."

Ophelia advanced, but Clyde hung back a moment, kicking off her shoes and shoving her socks inside them. Ophelia waited. Clyde picked her shoes up and advanced barefoot into the sand. She had square, straightforward toes, Ophelia noticed. Strong toes. Strong feet. Probably, callused. Probably, Clyde went barefoot all the time. She wouldn't try to take the train barefoot, but if she needed to walk two blocks to buy tamales from the guy on the corner, she wouldn't bother with shoes or sandals. I mean, why would she? She was Clyde!

Ophelia reluctantly shed her own shoes and socks. When her toes touched the sand, it felt like a dry kiss, cool and dark and reassuring. Summer hadn't left yet, but it had just started thinking about slipping away. The dull roar of the waves replaced the distant crush of traffic. There weren't any lights out on the lake. The City stretched for miles in every direction, but here it simply ended, full stop. You could wade into the lake and keep wading until the waves closed over your head.

"I can't swim," Ophelia said.

"You can't swim?" Clyde echoed. "How the hell you do a day on the beach if you can't swim?"

"I've never done a day at the beach."

"Aren't you from Michigan? Aren't there tons of beaches there?"

"Probably. I never got out to them much, though. I've been on pontoons. A couple paddle wheels."

Clyde kept moving down the beach.

The sand got cooler, turned wet, the wind sullen, and the waves surged around Ophelia's ankles.

"Jesus, that's cold!" she said.

Clyde laughed.

"Stop laughing," Ophelia said, but she was laughing too.

Clyde joined her in the surge, and they stood on the shore, looking outward, the waves rushing about their ankles.

"Is this where you saw the shark?" Clyde asked.

"I didn't tell you anything about a shark," said Ophelia.

"No, but you were talking to Ashley about it at the party, and then Ferin, too."

Ophelia squinted. The far horizon looked stoic and undisturbed. It seemed strange, now, to think that she could have seen a monstrosity out there. Yet her eyes had told her. The waves had hit her. The creature was real, and it had changed the trajectory of her night. Maybe of her life.

"Yeah," said Ophelia. "I saw it."

"I've known a few things. Extraterrestrials tapping on the door of my parents' motorhome. Promising me a real life if I would just leave home and go away with them. Telling me I could be in a country band. Go out west. Reno. Missoula. Gallup. I said no. I wasn't going to leave home and go out west or to Venus or ... or whatever. I left home and came to the City."

"You believe me," said Ophelia, and she took Clyde's hand.

"Everyone believes you," said Clyde.

They looked out for a long time. The waves rolled in on silver-frothed purple surges, turning gray as they hit the shore.

"I want to ask you two questions," said Clyde. "I don't know what order to ask them."

"It doesn't matter," said Ophelia.

She knew her voice sounded mute and expressionless. She felt naked and numb. She dreaded to desire. She dreaded disappointment.

"They are separate questions," said Clyde. "Your answer to one question doesn't have anything to do with the answer to the other."

"Ask away."

"Okay. First question. You said you have to leave and go back to Rockville tomorrow. And I said that Violent let me stay on her couch for months while I figured my shit out. Well, one good turn deserves another, right? You get some good, you pass it along, right? You want to stay with me? I can cover the rent; I'm already good on that for a while, and I can help you get a job at the hospital."

Nothing surprised Ophelia; she had so thoroughly stripped her mind of expectation.

"Yeah," she said. "I mean, thank you. I don't want to go. I want to stay."

"Great," said Clyde, nervously licking her lips.

"What's the other question?"

"Can I kiss you?"

〰〰〰〰〰

WHEN CLYDE AND OPHELIA MADE it back to the building with their spit mingled in Ophelia's mouth, they rode the elevator up to Clyde's sixth-floor apartment. Clyde then rubbed her sleepy eyes as she dragged out some clean but threadbare sheets and a homemade quilt. She tucked them with hospital corners onto a broken red couch she'd bought on Craigslist for fifty bucks— "They ripped me off on that one!"—and fluffed the pillow for Ophelia. Then Clyde went off to her bedroom, and Ophelia lay there with her eyes open. She saw a gray light growing upon the walls. Morning was coming at last.

The last day and night had turned everything upside down. When Ophelia had gotten off the Red Line at the Thorndale stop, she'd been expecting to share an apartment with Tasia, her life in the City mediated by friends and family and frequent trips back home. Now, twelve hours later, she was completely alone, felt completely new, as stunned as a newborn, wide-eyed with the dawn unobstructed upon that massive lake with all its sands and sharks. The sun rose, and Ophelia slept and smiled. The bad day had become a good day.

But this was the beginning, not the end, of Ophelia's time in the City.

WHEN OPHELIA WOKE THE NEXT afternoon, Clyde was already up and brushing her teeth. She dumped some cold coffee into a plastic thermos. They went up to Ophelia's apartment to gather her belongings, but Clyde stopped her as soon as she arrived.

"This is just like Stan and Ferin's place!"

"Yeah," said Ophelia. "They have the same floor plan."

"What did you pay for this?"

"Um, eight-fifty a month."

"Eight-fifty?! I pay six-eighty for mine, and it's like half this size!"

Clyde sat in the middle of the living room and looked out the windows to the high rises, now bright with daylight. She glared at a roach crawling along one of the baseboards.

"One of us has to break their lease," she said. "I think I should break mine. Move in here. I can cover the extra rent until you get a job. But this is, like, way better than my place."

Instead of taking one trip to bring Ophelia's luggage to the sixth floor, they spent the rest of the afternoon carting all of Clyde's bedding and clothes and books and cookware and the busted couch up the freight elevator to Ophelia's apartment.

"We can get my name on the lease if you like," Clyde said. "I don't know how we'll pull it, but I don't mind."

"It's okay," said Ophelia. "I trust you."

"Well, you better let me pay you upfront now. Because if you don't have cash, how you gonna get groceries or a bus pass to apply for jobs?"

"You don't have to. But. That's nice."

⟫⟫⟫⟫⟫

THEY PUT THE COUCH IN her bedroom since Ophelia didn't have a bed. Clyde took the larger bedroom. She wanted the lake view. She was happy to pay a bit extra for the privilege. She wrote Ophelia a check for five hundred dollars that night. Then Clyde cooked some black beans and rice with onions, and they ate and went up to see Ferin and Stan.

"Look who's staying a little longer!" she said.

"This deserves a toast," said Stan.

"We're out of wine," said Ferin.

"This deserves a cheap beer toast!" said Stan.

〉〉〉〉〉

WHEN MONDAY ROLLED AROUND, CLYDE took Ophelia to the Thorndale station, and they bought her a 30-day pass from the transit vending machine. Clyde held the card solemnly before Ophelia's face.

"This little magnetized card," she said, "is your key to this whole city. You can ride all the trains and, like, a hundred buses. You can go to Beverly, and you can go to Rogers Park. This city is literally a billion square miles, and now you get to see all of them."

Ophelia cradled the card in her palm as if it was a diamond.

"But the best is the 147 bus," said Clyde. "The 147 gets you downtown in like 30 minutes during rush hour."

〉〉〉〉〉

THE NEXT MORNING, THEY BOUGHT scrambled eggs and watery coffee from the Cambodian man in the subterranean restaurant beneath the El tracks, the crumbling concrete walls shivering whenever a train passed overhead. They walked back to Sheridan with its glittering windows and jumped onto the 147 bus, double-length, joined by some rough accordion plastic in the middle, and it whirred almost ten miles south with the high-rises to the right and the lake to the left. As they advanced, the battlemented ranks of the downtown skyscrapers advanced, ever so slowly, any one of its buildings a maw fit to devour the tallest structures left in Rockville. Ophelia looked out to the lake and scanned its white-capped waves for signs of the shark. She saw none. Where did you go? she wondered. What do you want?

But soon, she was distracted by the double-decker bascule bridge, its metal lattice offering glimpses of hundreds—*thousands?*—of vehicles flowing north and south just beneath the bus and all its friends and a few boats passing on the water below. Now, the river briefly parted the towers into a canyon of long shadows falling steely across the sun-diamonded choppy waves.

They disembarked into throngs of humans and walked ten minutes to the temp agency across the street from Clyde's hospital. The lobby inside was windowless, with beige walls and ugly carpet. Ophelia filled out the forms, interviewed with a woman with perfect blonde hair, cut along the shoulders with mortarboard precision, and said, "I'll work anywhere. Really."

"Will you dress up like a bear and hand out surveys at Soldier Field?" the woman asked.

Ophelia stilled.

"Then don't say anywhere," the woman said.

"What? No, I mean, yes. Of course, I will."

A few minutes later, Clyde told her, "No, you won't. You're going to wear khakis and Oxford white dress shirts and work clerical in neurosurgery or ophthalmology or orthopedics or reproductive endocrinology."

She dragged Ophelia across the street and into the hospital, plated with huge windows and gleaming walls soaring skyward.

"What if they don't call me?" asked Ophelia.

"They'll call you," Clyde said. "You're attentive and polite. They always need file clerks. Trust me."

The next day, the agency called. They offered Ophelia $10.60 an hour; not a lot, but more than she had ever earned at any job before, and anyway, it was all hers.

ᗡᗡᗡᗡᗡ

THE DAYS CAME BUSY AND fast. Each morning brought new responsibilities. One day, Ophelia took the bus downtown alone and bought the khakis and Oxford shirts the hospital required. She bought a bagel and coffee from a little Greek restaurant, then went back to the temp agency to take her HIPAA training and test for Microsoft Office. Now, she was ready for work at the hospital's Lasik center. It was on the fourteenth floor, with views of the lake and the northern skyline.

The next day, she walked to a grimy thrift store surrounded by public housing and decommissioned mental hospitals and bought herself some blouses and blankets. Now she could show up at Stan and Ferin's parties in a low-key style of her own.

The day after that, Ophelia and Clyde walked a block to the east—"People's income goes up by like 50K every block you get closer to the lake."—and scoured the alleys for discarded furniture. They returned home with two leather-upholstered desk chairs, their green paint chipping but loaded with the stories of a dozen asses. On their next trip, they brought home a dozen milk crates and a file cabinet with the key still dangling from the lock. Next, an all-metal desk scrapped by some USPS office. Ophelia thought she was going to throw out her back, wrestling that thing into the elevator. As she was setting up her room, she heard a voice calling out her name:

"Hey! Hey Ophelia!"

It was Clyde, but Clyde wasn't there. The voice rayed in through the open window. Ophelia stuck her head out and looked down.

"No, up here! Up here!"

Ophelia looked across the angle of the building, where she saw a tiny window looking into the bathroom and shower. Clyde's face was pressed up against the screen.

"I'm naked in here!" Clyde yelled.

Ophelia laughed and shut her window.

She kept cleaning.

♪♪♪♪♪

THE NIGHTS WERE AS BUSY as the days.

Some nights, Clyde and Ophelia stayed in and worked puzzles or played games on Clyde's Nintendo emulator. Clyde had lost her internet after moving out of Violentina's apartment, so no email, no Blogspot, no MySpace or Facebook.

And some nights, Ophelia wanted to write her brother, so she'd go down to the Nigerian Internet Cafe, but she got sick of the same gross-smelling redneck browsing porn there all hours. And sometimes, Violentina came over and brought her Alfred Hitchcock DVDs, and they'd watch *The 39 Steps* or *North by Northwest* or *Vertigo* while eating Ramen or popcorn.

On other nights, they'd go up to Stan and Ferin's, and those nights usually ran late. Stan and Ferin always left their apartment unlocked. Sometimes, Ophelia discovered the door hanging open, trailing noisy drum'n'bass out into the hall. When she went inside, she might find Stan tricking out his computers with more lights and decals or Ferin hunched over a notebook, scribbling pictures and poetry with runic abandon. Sometimes Angel came over, or Ashley, or Brendan, or everyone all together, and then there was always spaghetti and beer and rum and loud music. Ophelia stopped hating the heaving booming from overhead. She knew it meant that her neighbors were home again.

They threw a party every week. None of these were as complex or choreographed as the night Ophelia had moved to the City, though Ferin and Olivia often went off to the kitchen to whisper darkly about plans for the next event. Everyone else seemed content to dance in the living room in the glow of the lake and Sheridan Road, and the carpet muffled the sound of their feet.

These were moments when Ophelia stood apart from her new friends, looking out the windows from between the clunky computer monitors. The lake was out there, always, pressed between the high rises, and its color changed depending on when Ophelia was looking. On a chilly morning, with the clouds sparse, the lake spoke through the sun, reflecting gem sparkles, turquenite, lazurite, aquamarine. On a windy afternoon, when heavy waves in shallow water churned the sand and seaweed into a froth, the water looked like moss. When the weather turned toward autumn and darkness, the waves marched in steel ranks wearing helms plumed with cold white feathers. And at night, it was ink, pitch, tar, a starless sky.

"What is my shark doing?" Ophelia asked in those moments.

She was speaking to herself, but not softly, and so someone always answered. Whoever was standing nearby. They spoke to understand and reassure her.

"Maybe you'll never see it again," said Angel. "Maybe it appeared just that once so you could know you belonged here."

"I don't think it speaks the same language that we do," Ferin said. "Sharks are hundreds of millions of years old. They know what we do not. It's more likely to know our ways than we are to know its ways."

"Do you think it stayed here?" asked Olivia. "Maybe it migrated to the north. Maybe it was just visiting for breeding, or food, or hibernation, and now it's made its way on."

"I think it wants to destroy this city," said Violentina.

Ophelia smiled and nodded but thought they had it all wrong. She knew it was foolish to try and guess at the shark's motives. Her fear, at its first appearance, had dissolved into a hushed awe. It appeared, she thought. Everything was horrible, and then my shark appeared, and then everything became wonderful.

"I don't understand it either," said Clyde, as if she had opened a backdoor to Ophelia's mind and read her thoughts in silent songs.

It made Ophelia want to cry, and she took Clyde's hand and squeezed it until she gasped from the pressure.

〜〜〜〜

Two weeks after Ophelia had arrived in City, she came home to find the apartment steeped in a briny, pungent, curdled smell.

"Check it out!" said Clyde, leading her into the kitchen. "I'm making chicha!" She lifted the lid off a pot, and the thick scent wafted deeper through the room.

"What is that?" asked Ophelia.

"Fermented corn beer. The Incans brewed it all the time. I'm not sure I'm doing it right, though."

Ophelia saw some shredded corn mush floating in the stagnant water.

Clyde put the lid back down.

"Clyde, I wanted to ask you," Ophelia said. "I've been thinking about this all day today. And I'm really happy right now. I feel so lucky. And so busy. I feel happy, but I can't stop moving, you know? Anyway, I wanted to ask you. You kissed me on the night of the first party. But you haven't asked me to kiss you since then."

"I know I haven't," Clyde said.

Ophelia's heart started pounding. "Why? I mean, no pressure or anything, but ... why?"

"Because you haven't had any money. You didn't have a job. You just got here. Because ... you were depending on me for a lot ... when you first got here. I didn't think it was fair to you. I didn't want you to feel any pressure ... to go along with me ... and I didn't want what I felt to get messed up when what I needed to do was help you out. Like, I didn't want you to feel like you needed to depend on me."

"I like depending on you," Ophelia said. "Okay. But how do you feel about me?"

"You excite me. You listen to me. Every night I lie there and think about you sleeping on that shitty couch in your room—"

"Kiss me," Ophelia said.

They kissed.

That night, Ophelia shared Clyde's queen-sized bed.

〉〉〉〉〉〉

THE LEAVES FELL. OPHELIA'S BLISS deepened. Gradually, though, she realized that a gloom was troubling her friends upstairs. It was bothering Clyde, too.

"What's wrong?" she asked, sitting at the table with dirty dinner dishes spread about.

Clyde was scowling at the Reader.

"That fucker Bush is probably gonna win," she said. "After he all but stole the last election. After he fucked up the response to 9/11. After landing us in this terrible war!"

So, it was politics bothering her friends. Politics bothered her dad, too. The Democrats enraged him, and so he voted for Republicans. The Republicans enraged her brother, so he voted for Democrats. "Don't vote for that loser," they both told her, so she didn't. She figured her grandma understood. During the last election, Ophelia remembered when someone had referred to the candidates as "Gush" and "Bore." That had made her laugh.

"Does it even matter?" she asked Clyde.

"What?!" said Clyde.

"I mean, aren't they pretty much the same?" she said.

"Jesus, Ophelia. Do they both suck, yeah, I guess? Are they the same, hell no! Who sent us to war? Who's responsible for torturing prisoners? Who's responsible for what happened at Abu Graib?!"

Ophelia didn't know about the last two questions, but she understood the first and figured Clyde was probably backing the challenger.

"Bush?" she said.

"Fuck yeah, Bush! Fuck that fucking moron!"

At that moment, Clyde reminded Ophelia of her brother. He had the quickest tongue of anyone she knew, but when her brother spoke of the people who had injured his family, his blue eyes cleared, and his voice trembled softly. She didn't trust his judgment, though. Despite her love for Clyde, Ophelia wasn't sure she trusted her judgment.

"Okay," she said. "But can you really say things would have been better if Gore had been won?"

"Good, probably not, but better than right now, hell yeah! Would we be at war? I don't know. But I don't think we'd be torturing people. I don't think we'd have these assholey tax cuts. And then there's the whole DOMA bullshit. I don't know, I honestly have no idea, how you, a queer woman in America today, can act like there's no difference between Bush and Kerry!"

Yeah, Clyde was pissed. Her certainty hardened with probing. At the same time, almost everyone in Rockville who voted voted Democratic, and Ophelia knew plenty of those people who had called her brother a fag. All the times they'd given him shit at the bus stop. It angered her then, and it angered her now. His conviction had never diminished her anger.

"What are you thinking?" Clyde asked, her face flushed.

"That's what," said Ophelia. "I'm thinking. Let me think, okay?"

Am I even *a queer woman?* she wondered. She'd never used the words to describe herself. I was with Andre a bunch of times. It was ... alright. And he got me pregnant. How many lesbians get pregnant? Now she was probing herself instead of Clyde: Why shouldn't they get pregnant? What should getting pregnant have to do with whether I'm 'queer' or not. Whether I'm... a lesbian.

Clyde kept staring. Her face was getting redder and redder. Not with rage, Ophelia realized, but with impatience. She wasn't used to giving or accepting silence.

It was okay with Andre. I guess. But not like it was with Tasia. Not like I was awake all over. Not like it is with Clyde. Not like I am now, alive all over. Awake! Alive! Holy fuck, I'm a lesbian!

As the realization broke over her like the waves of the lake, the shock of the moment, combined with Clyde's tomatoing face, and mirth bubbled up within Ophelia and exploded in peals of laughter.

"What the hell is it?" Clyde sounded angry even though Ophelia knew this was nothing more or less than confusion.

"My dad," Ophelia gasped. "He's such a fuckup. He doesn't like gays, though. But he's got two gay kids!"

She was laughing so hard that she felt tears on her cheek.

"You didn't know that?" burst Clyde.

Ophelia shrugged happily. "I just figured I was Clydesexual."

"Well, more people should be,' said Clyde.

When Ophelia had recovered her breath, she rested her hands on Clyde's. "Tell me about the election," she said. "I want to understand better."

"Okay," said Clyde. "But I'm getting some Doritos first. I'm still fucking starving."

⁂

OPHELIA REGISTERED TO VOTE ON the last possible day before the election. On November 2nd, she walked through the icy rain to the elementary school across from the El stop. The puddles soaked her shoes, but she went into the gym and voted for the first time in her life.

That night, everyone came over to Stan and Ferin's apartment. A lot of them were late; they'd been getting the vote out until long after the sun had set and arrived cold and damp. Angel had planned this party, taking advantage of Ferin's larger kitchen. She hummed softly as she cooked, frying pancakes, hash browns, eggs, and bacon. Everyone drank beer and sipped coffee and watched the results start to come in. The mood in the room had started out gloomy and it sank deeper as each state was announced. As the map gradually filled with red, Ophelia's friends bid goodbye, one by one. Eventually, everyone had left except Stan, Ferin, Angel, Brendan, Clyde, and Violent.

"At least Illinois and Michigan didn't disappoint us," Ferin mumbled as he piled dirty dishes in the sink.

"Fuck this country!" snapped Clyde. "I was out in that rain for hours tonight. I don't think I got anyone to vote!"

"You got someone to vote," said Ophelia.

"I hear you, I appreciate you. But Illinois was gonna go blue anyway. If I really cared, I should've gone to Iowa."

It was a sad night, but Ophelia's heart grew with every person and every thing she started to care about. The people she had grown up with. The people she had discovered. The place she had left and the place they had arrived. She cared for all of them now, and each time she learned to care, she felt herself becoming larger, her voice stronger, her purpose clearer. She had already outgrown the shell of someone who thought "politics don't matter."

〰〰〰〰〰

DRAB RAIN FELL FOR DAYS after the election. Eventually, a gray wind came through and stripped the last of the leaves from the trees. Ophelia didn't make it down to the beach much anymore, though she still stood near the radiators and studied the lake for signs of her shark. Instead of receding into the haze of memory, its form became ever more distinct and real, even in its absence. She felt the dull red eyes, watching her, impassive, the great teeth towering within its monstrous mouth, its silence, and then the future of its wake as it plowed the waves to shore. She longed for it. She felt the transformation it had wrought in her. She wished it well.

Upstairs, the election had only briefly dampened Ferin's enthusiasm. By the next night, he'd sent out an invitation to an emergency party that Friday. He was inviting all of the nations to his living room. Azerbaijan's invitation went by email. Canada's was dropped in the mailbox. Several nations had to rest content with Facebook posts but were nonetheless invited. When the party finally convened, with the sun finally breaking through the clouds, the nations were no-shows, but Ferin, Stan, Olivia, Angel, Ashley, Brendan, Colm, Eliza, Violentina, Clyde, Ophelia, and a DJ named Aley Hoofddorp made it on time.

Ferin and Olivia outlined the vision: Five more parties, and this would be the first. The parties would provide everything a party was meant to provide: food, dancing, games, conversation, and joy. Also, the parties would provide everything a party was meant to provide: representation, a platform, money, and clout. The parties would be organized and funded by the Hollywood Group. What was the Hollywood Group? It was everyone present in that living room. Everyone who had consecrated themselves that year through windows looking out over Hollywood Beach.

Since that night's party was the first of the Party parties, they had to make it count. So, they volunteered to do what they'd love. Stan was on music. Angel was on food. Brendan promised to scoop out the good booze. Olivia would organize lights, art, and visual effects. Ferin would write the mysteries and create the games. Ashley knew some bands and musicians and said she'd try to hook them up with some live acts. Aley said he'd spin for them. He'd left Marquette with three computers, and while they were individually shitty, he was pretty sure he could combine them into something workable. The others volunteered to clean, promote, and run errands. Where would it all lead? Ferin seemed to think it would take them to the moon. Angel had her doubts, but she felt like it might at least be fun.

As it got darker outside and brighter in the room, their hopes started to lift, lilt, and finally soar. The black coffee and cheap beer enhanced their desires and solidarities. There were nostalgic souls in that room—Andy Kaufman devotees—and since his mission had seemed similar in spirit to theirs, Brendan and Angel whipped up some screwdrivers while the rest took turns proclaiming from The Great Gatsby. By one in the morning, they'd finished the vodka, though Daisy and Jay hadn't yet consummated their affair, and everyone slipped off to their own apartments, or the couches, or the floor. The Hollywood Group had been born, and Ophelia felt certain that, somewhere, the shark smiled upon them.

※※※※※

NOW WINTER ADVANCED. THE LAST of the Halloween decorations came down and Christmas lights went up.

Ophelia arrived at the hospital before the sun had ever crested the horizon and watched as it shifted overhead and sank and set before she had even punched out for the night. Autumn had been brisk business at the Lasik center, and Ophelia kept busy as she learned the nuances of chart organization, and how each of the four doctors wanted their materials prepared, and how long to wait before marking a late patient as a No Show, and that the coffee in the 19th-floor staff lounge was undrinkable sludge. Now, business seemed to taper off. Post-Thanksgiving, everyone was too busy to get eye surgery.

"Just wait until January," her manager said. "They'll all be dipping into their flex spending accounts before they lapse for the year. You won't get a chance to sit down!"

The Ophthalmology Department held a holiday party at a downtown hotel, and Ophelia brought Clyde, who dressed in a suit and tie. Between them, they drank so much rum punch that they fell asleep on the Red Line going home, and woke up at the end of the line, with the station attendant tapping irritably at their window.

"Tomorrow, we're going to regret that," Clyde said.

Ophelia nodded a sludgy answer.

But the next night, the Hollywood Group convened the second of their five parties at Olivia's apartment on the South Side. The costumed partiers descended upon Hyde Park wearing fur coats and Hawai'ian shirts, floral shawls and gauzy dresses, plaid skirts and shaded sunglasses. They drank tea and ate sweets. Olivia's sister Pearl and her boyfriend sat on the couch, chewing on apples, and bemusedly took in the chaos around them. Eventually,

Ferin invited the other guests into a small parlor for Tarot readings while Angel, Ashley, and Olivia sketched chalk renderings of the surreal prognostications. Any political conversation was strictly in the abstract. Any activism was firmly in the future tense. And yet, the Hollywood Group proliferated ideas of a quantity that obliterated any deficiencies in quality. It didn't matter how much of it was soot and stamp sand; somewhere in that quarry hid gemstones.

And so, Ashley fantasized about moving to San Francisco and starting painting again. Eliza wanted to resume her work on tropical diseases, even if it landed her in Suriname for months. Ferin and Angel had gotten engaged. He was applying to grad schools now for writing. She was weighing out the pros and cons of nursing and social work. Brendan wanted to brew his own beer, and Stan dreamed of one day getting a van and making it into a movable house. Clyde wanted some Scooby-Doo DVDs. She thought she might take up knitting. Ophelia remembered that she had run the sound on a play once in high school and thought it might be fun to audition now.

It was a good night.

ת ת ת ת ת

IT NEEDED TO BE GOOD. The following day, Ophelia said goodbye to Clyde for two weeks and boarded the train to Rockville. After a six-hour ride, she climbed into a chilly, drab afternoon, walked down to Ash Highway, and waited for her half-sister to pick her up.

The days that followed were a pleasant and hazy dream. Most of Ophelia's family was not doing noticeably worse, though everyone was concerned about her brother and her dad. Neither of them was anywhere to be seen, and the messages left for them went unreturned. A few more houses on Ophelia's grandparents' block had gone abandoned. A few more of the factories had closed, so now only a couple were left. But the coneys were spicy, the smiles genuine, and the backyards had space and grass and lilacs, and were able to breathe in ways that the tiny lots in the City could not. On Christmas morning, Santa-with-her-grandma's-handwriting had left a check for five hundred dollars made out to Ophelia. She thought she might start saving for a car.

On the day after Christmas, she went down to Spencer's at the mall and spent an hour talking to Tasia. It felt awkward for a few minutes. Tasia kept apologizing, and Ophelia kept "Don't worry"ing. But soon, her friend was piling her arms with discounted earrings and trinkets, and they were laughing about the confused dads window shopping outside.

"You gonna join us for New Year's Eve?" Tasia asked.

"You know it," said Ophelia.

"We'll get the oldest champagne, just like Jimmy Stewart and Donna Reed."

"You mean the cheapest champagne!"

"What was it Letterman said? Nasti Spumanti?"

"White Trashfendel!"

"I Can't Believe It's Not Vinegar!"

They laughed and laughed.

"You know," Ophelia said, pressing deeper into the moment, into the remembrance of trust with this person who had helped retrieve her from the worst days. "I thought I was in love with you."

"With me?"

"Yeah. I did." She laughed.

"Jesus!" said Tasia. "Is that because of ... the 4th of July?"

"Uh-huh."

"I didn't mean to ..... I just thought that was, you know, the alcohol."

"The alcohol didn't hurt. But it opened a door, you know. I like girls. I had that inside me. That and so much more. I took it all to the city with me, and I met a friend there, and the friend opened the door, and it all spilled out and into the world!"

Tasia watched her with amazement.

"Do you like it then?" she asked. "The city? Your apartment? Your girlfriend? Your new life there?"

"Yeah," said Ophelia. "I love it. I'm hopeful, you know?"

"Hopeful there. Not like here. Hopeless."

"Not hopeless. There's hope here, too."

"When you find it, you let me know."

They fell into silence then. Ophelia wasn't sure whether Tasia wasn't bitter or joking. Then Tasia winked, and it was both at once.

"We'll get you good and drunk on New Year's Eve," she said. "Rockville style. Just don't have a go at me, or we'll have you on Shirley Temples next time."

"I ain't a two-timer!" Ophelia answered.

They watched each other for a moment.

"Can I just walk out of here with these earrings," Ophelia asked.

"You remember how the last manager got sacked?" asked Tasia. "Sheee-it."

〉〉〉〉〉

HALFWAY AROUND THE WORLD, A great wave obliterated the lives of a million people. In the Midwest, fuzzy snowflakes had long since replaced rain and falling leaves. On the train ride back to the City, Ophelia watched as drop after drop of water streaked down her window, only to freeze in place before reaching the bottom.

She stood at the window for a long time in her apartment. Warmth and amber filled the high-rises, while vapor chugged from all the vents like vapor heating the inky night, but the beach was barren and lifeless. Moldy clumps of congealed snow crusted the water. Ophelia hoped her shark was safe and comfortable.

〉〉〉〉〉

IT WASN'T LONG BEFORE THE Hollywood Group had reassembled from their holiday peregrinations. In the dark and cold of the New Year—2005—they threw two more parties in quick succession.

The third party was probably Ophelia's favorite of them all. Unlike the others, it hadn't been meticulously planned around elaborate plots and intricate imagery. This happening was simply a surfeit of light on a bitterly cold night, and it ran all night long. The word of these events had gotten out, in some small way, because people kept arriving long after all of the Hollywood Group had made an appearance. There might have been thirty people crammed into Stan and Ferin's apartment that night, or there might have been fifty. Eleven o'clock passed, then midnight, and then one, and just when it seemed like things might be starting to wind down, Ashley stepped through the door with a mariachi band right behind her, and the music and dancing started anew.

The fourth party was the one that got out of hand. Mardi Gras themed, it launched in the late afternoon when Brendan exploited a promotional deal at a bar on Rush Street, and the snotty bartenders sullenly sloughed up weak rum cokes in exchange for many one-dollar tips. After several cocktails before the sun went down, the crowd stumbled and swore on the train ride back to the apartment. Aley almost pitched himself into the elevator shaft when the doors opened with the car suspended a half-floor above him. Inside, dancing quickly devolved into spin-the-bottle, but Clyde and Ophelia slipped out then. They reserved their caresses for each other.

The mornings after these parties—and many other mornings—any Hollywoodites scattered across the apartment building—the beds and couches and carpeted floors—stomped through the salt and the whistling wind to a diner for breakfast. They nursed their hangovers with dry scrambled eggs and orange juice and fed their ambitions.

"I think I might run for Board of Education," said Benthia. She was a newcomer. She'd arrived at Party #3 and, by Party #4, had hooked up with Brendan. She had inducted herself into the group as seamlessly as had Ophelia. So had Eugene, a friend of Ferin's obsessed with country music and New Wave.

"Someday, I want to audition for a play," said Ophelia.

༄༄༄༄༄

AS THE DAYS GREW LONGER and the wind started to flow from the east, Ophelia found herself pacing through the chilly apartment barefoot, feeling sad and baffled by the ever-growing immensity of her life. The lake had thawed, but its horizons looked more desolate than ever. The sidewalks were still bitterly cold and empty, and green things had not yet emerged.

One night, Stan and Violentina took Clyde to an Infected Mushroom concert, and Ophelia had the place to herself. The post-holiday flurry of busyness at the clinic had fallen into a slump these last few weeks; the four doctors were surly with neglect, and Ophelia's manager had said the word "layoffs." Still, Ophelia felt tired and defeated after she got home. She felt lonelier and more disconnected than she had in months. She dragged her sleeping bag out of the closet and wrapped herself up on the broken couch in her bedroom. It got dark outside, but Ophelia didn't stir. She fell into an uneasy sleep.

She woke hours later into a suffocating dread. Panic wept in the cloudy shadows on every side. Panic hung by webs across her windows. Panic was in the impossibly distant light of the living room, at the end of the hall, where someone had left a lamp on all night long. *But what woke me?*

Then the scream repeated. It was coming from the apartment across the hall. Ophelia was certain of it. The direction of the voice? It couldn't have come from anywhere. It was a young and frenzied female voice, and the voice was panic, and the voice was pain. Someone was stabbing the screamer with something sharp. The voice rang out so clear, so immediate, that Ophelia knew that she had forgotten to close the door to the apartment when she had gotten home that night. Like Stan and Ferin, she had left the door hanging wide for her friends to enter and relax, but this time it wouldn't be a friend answering the invitation.

What do I do? she wondered.

I should call for help, she thought.

But the phone was in the living room, and the living room was lighted, and the living room was right around the corner from that open door, from that hall, from the murder being committed at that very moment.

If I go out there, they'll hear me walking, or they'll hear my voice, and they'll murder me too. Even though I should do something. Even though I should help.

Ophelia retreated into the darkest, most secretive corner of her bedroom. When you've grown up afraid, you hide when you can. She huddled with her eyes wide open and waited for the screaming to stop.

Eventually, she woke up in her bed again. So, I dreamed it, after all, she thought. The sky was starting to turn purple outside. Ophelia slipped on her nightgown and went to the kitchen to grab a couple cookies. She stopped dead in the living room on her way back to her room. The front door hung open. The flickering fluorescent light from the hall bathed the entrance a sickly green.

"Clyde?" Ophelia called out nervously.

No one answered.

She hurried to Clyde's room and flicked the light on. The bed was empty, its covers undisturbed. Ophelia was still alone.

What was the dream? Ophelia fretted. What was real?

She peeked into the empty hall and looked all the way down to the fire escape. She crossed the hall and started banging on the opposite door. She banged and banged and banged and finally heard someone cursing on the other side.

The door opened a sliver, and Ophelia saw an older man and a younger man, both sleepy-eyed, glaring out at her.

"What?" the older man said. "What?"

"Are you okay?" Ophelia asked. "I thought ... I thought maybe there was trouble here. I thought maybe that."

The old man glared harder, and the young man watched Ophelia with disbelieving scorn.

Who are you? their faces said. Why are you here?

Ophelia backed away from them. She opened the door to the stairs. She was running down. She wouldn't look over her shoulder. She was running as fast as she could.

〽〽〽〽〽

OPHELIA LOST PANTING MOMENTS, THEN. Her mind stood outside her body, wreathed in fog, and she didn't know the time. She knew that she was changing. Those places were changing. Cold was growing. Then she returned to her body and realized she was standing on Hollywood Beach, right at the water's edge. Icy gray waves ran up between her toes and shocked her nerves. Ophelia looked out across the lake. The clouds ahead had gathered in preparation for the dawn, but the water rolled on as ever. The buoy bounced, but there was nothing else to see.

"Where did you go?" Ophelia shouted. "Why did you leave me? What did you want? Why can't I see you?"

She was certain that nobody could hear her cries. That the lake and sky alone witnessed her in those moments. But then, to her astonishment, a monstrous proliferation of bubbles began to percolate upwards. Far away and immeasurably large, the shark surfaced. But it was different this time. Its skin had turned pale and leathery while its belly was bloated with gas. A milky film covered its bloodshot eyes. The stiffened shark did not hold itself upright as it had before, but once the lake had raised it to the surface, the creature rolled onto its side. As the wake flowed out, a noxious cloud of decomposition followed.

The creature was dead, and again, as Ophelia doubted the truth that her eyes had told her, the waves came upon her and reminded her of reality. She was drenched, her own fingers and toes numb and pale, her teeth chattering as the sun prepared to rise.

〰〰〰

WHEN OPHELIA MADE IT BACK to the apartment, she heard Clyde before she saw her. The door was hanging open, just as Ophelia had left it, and she went inside. Stan and Violentina stood in the living room and turned toward the door as Ophelia entered.

"Holy shizballs!" said Stan.

Ophelia looked down at herself and realized she looked half-drowned, half-frozen. She couldn't say anything, though. She was still shivering too hard.

Clyde had yet to hear. She held the phone to her ear and was looking out the window.

"No, I just want you to call around and tell me if you can find—"

"Um, Clyde," said Violentina, and she tugged on Clyde's sleeve.

Clyde turned and saw Ophelia. She didn't flinch.

"You know, never mind," said Clyde and hung up the phone. She put it back on the scavenged end table.

"Are you okay?" she asked.

Ophelia nodded.

"What happened?" Clyde asked.

Ophelia started to cry.

"Guys, thanks, really, great night. Get some sleep."

Stan and Violentina shouldered their coats with understanding nods and left, closing the door behind them.

"Babe, what happened?"

Stuttering, too cold to talk, Ophelia pointed weakly toward the window.

"Shh," said Clyde. "You need a warm bath. And some tea. And some soup."

꙳꙳꙳꙳꙳

CLYDE DREW THE BATH. CLYDE steeped the tea. Clyde warmed the Ramen in the skillet and brought it on a wood plank to serve as a tray. She'd bought a discounted bowl in Chinatown, and it was white, smooth as an egg, and undecorated.

As the warmth of the water flowed into her bones, Ophelia's teeth stopped chattering. She sipped the tea first, then the soup, while Clyde washed her hair. Ophelia became fixated upon the tips of her toes sticking out from the water at the bottom of the shallow tub. Her toes were the last part of her to warm.

The cold finally left her when she realized Clyde was not in the room anymore. Panic shot her. She called out, "Clyde?!"

Clyde returned, unruffled, reassuring. She carried a brownie on a small plate.

"You seem to be doing better," she said. "And I've just had one hell of a night. So, here's what I think. We're going to enjoy this delicious edible, and you tell me what the fuck happened while I was gone."

Ophelia nodded gratefully. She took half of the brownie in her hand, cradling it so as not to drop a single precious crumb into the soapy water. She ate it in a single bite.

Slowly—haltingly—Ophelia told Clyde about her night. About the nightmare of the murder. About the reality of the open door. About the waking dream on Hollywood Beach.

"But I know it's real because I was soaked when I came back."

"Hell yeah, you were," said Clyde. "I'm glad you didn't drown or die of hypothermia. I don't know what to do about all this, but I know one thing. We've got to teach you how to swim. Maybe we wait until it gets a bit warmer out, or maybe we sign you up at the YMCA, but if you're gonna go chasing sharks in the lake in March, you'd better know how to swim."

"Do you really think it's dead?"

"I believed you when you said it was alive, so why would I doubt you when you say it's dead? You say you saw it, so you must have seen it. But maybe someday it'll be alive again. Maybe it isn't bound by life and death like we are."

"Why do you think it only appears to me? It's so huge. Is it really possible that I'm the only person who sees it?"

"I don't know anyone else who has seen it. I don't know why it's only appeared to you. But I'm sure it's got a good reason."

"There's good in Rockville, but I don't want to go back there. I want to stay here. I want to be here with you."

"I want you here with me, too."

By now, the brownie was kicking in. The pale bathroom pastels—pinks and whites—had started to grow close and lovely and comforting, and Ophelia felt a great tiredness flow across her. Clyde helped Ophelia from the bath, dried her, and gave her a pair of flannel pajamas. She led Ophelia into her bedroom with the pale light of March growing through the curtains and tucked her into the bed.

"Please don't leave me," said Ophelia. "I want you by my side right now."

"Are you kidding?" said Clyde. "I just spent the whole night dancing, and now I'm high and caffeinated. You sleep. I'm just going to lie here and read until I drift off."

The last thing Ophelia saw before she fell asleep was Clyde sipping her tea and reading the intro to What's the Matter with Kansas? The small lamp crowned her head with a halo.

〰〰〰〰〰

IN THE FOLLOWING WEEKS, OPHELIA recovered from her nightmare and the shock of the dead shark.

Distractions were everywhere. Olivia was part of a monumental production of Carmina Burana, and the whole Hollywood crew came out to support her, goggling at the peasants and nobles and stars and comets rocketing across the woven stage set. An even brighter spirit carried Ophelia down to the South Side with Clyde and Brendan for the St. Patrick's Day Parade. They watched a crowd of 20-something dudes shotgun Solo cups of green beer as flatbed trucks passed, filled with ranks of line-dancing teens.

But something in Ophelia's stomach hadn't settled since the night of her dreams. She still looked out the window at the lake. She no longer wondered what was living out of sight but worried about what corpse lay rotting at the bottom. She couldn't stop thinking that the water must now be unclean. She closed her eyes and tried to count the creatures poisoned by the decomposing flesh of her favorite monster. She feared what flowed from the tap.

With time, rain replaced the snow. The days surpassed the nights by length. The clouds descended and curled in soupy banks among the tight-pressed streets. The Hollywood Group converged for jazz under the dizzy lights of the Heartland Cafe. Benthia fell, running through the rain, and she looked so comical, the way her hands flapped up, like a mime trying to catch herself against mere air, that Clyde busted up laughing. Her heart stopped a moment later when Benthia stood up, a gash marring her palm from pinky to wrist and the rain swirling spirals of mud and blood.

On another obscure evening, Stan, Brendan, Benthia, and Ophelia sat in the warm glow of the Indonesian coffee shop, arguing about Nikola Tesla and the availability of free energy, but they all ended up crying from the sting of onion heels getting mauled by blunt-bladed knives in the kitchen.

The friends laughed about all these things. By now, their comfort and understanding ran deep. They knew and trusted each other. Still, it had been more than a month since the last of the Hollywood Parties, and nobody seemed to be planning the fifth and final event.

"Why?" Ophelia asked Clyde one night as she did the dishes.

"We're all a bit busy for parties." Clyde held up her soapy hands. "Haven't you noticed? Everything's moving now. Angel and Ferin are planning their wedding. They're moving to New Orleans or New York. Olivia's thinking she might head out to London again. Stan's planning to get a place with Aley and Brendan on the West Side. Shoot, maybe we should think about moving. I don't want to be the only one left out."

"I wish everyone would just stay here," Ophelia said. She felt her voice catch with resentment. "I wish we could all stay where we are. Why does anyone want to move? Where could be better than right here?"

THE NEXT TIME OPHELIA TOOK a call from Rockville—her dad was recovering from a weeklong bender, and her brother was high beyond the stratosphere—she told Clyde that she didn't think she could wait for the next train. Clyde told Ferin, and Ferin told Olivia and Olivia's father flew Ophelia to Saginaw in a Grumman Tiger. Rockville and other Michigan cities didn't look so awful from such heights. They were sullen constellations of yellow light, far enough down that their individual stars blurred, molten, and hopeful, and far enough apart that a new galaxy emerged on one horizon just as the last was vanishing behind her.

But after she touched the earth, the rest of the visit was red eyes, bitter thoughts, anxious words, and congestion. Ophelia polished off a pack of cigarettes, but she kept herself to one 40 a day while her grandma waved the phone in hand, checking in on her dad and looking for her brother. Her brother turned up. Her dad pulled through. Everyone was splitting weariness and headaches.

"That city of yours has changed you. All those dollars. Cents. Don't know how you can afford to live even," her grandma said, "but when he dies, I sure hope you'll come back for the funeral."

Ophelia stared at the carpet and her feet, then. She wasn't sure if her grandma was talking about her dad or brother. She loved them both. She couldn't do anything for them here. It was maddening, passing through the air—like an angel—only to sit on her grandma's couch, useless, surrounded by gray and despair. If either her dad or her brother died, of course, she'd come back, but it's not like they'd know. That, too, would be useless.

On Sunday morning, Ophelia returned to the abandoned playground where she'd once gone drinking with Lacey and Tasia. She sat on the busted merry-go-round, slowly spun, slowly sipped her Cobra, and looked into the bland and unforgiving sky. This was where Andre had tattooed her ankle. He'd used a sewing needle and a ballpoint pen. He had inked a passable dagger, but with time, it had blurred and became a drunken comma. A better symbol for what life here was, she thought. It isn't hopeless, but it isn't hopeful for me.

At the Amtrak station, Ophelia remembered to give her grandma the number for her new cell phone before heading home.

"Call me," Ophelia said. "If things get bad with either of them."

"If I call, you gonna pick up?" her grandma asked.

Ophelia strained and looked down the tracks for any sign of the train.

The leaves were heavy with buds now, but she couldn't wait to get out of there.

〉〉〉〉〉

ONE MORNING, OLIVIA WOKE LATE because her manager had told her not to come in until noon. Only three patients had scheduled appointments that day. She slouched out to the kitchen in her fuzzy bathrobe, alone because Clyde had already left for the day. Ophelia turned on the radio—all blues, all day long, revering music and sounds that other places had subsumed or forgotten—and looked out at the lake. Seven stories down, the trees had finally sprung; the maple buds erupting like miniature green fireworks, the delicate catalpa buds, more tentative, delicate, drooping with promises of swords and violence.

If the shark was dead, it was gone. If the shark was alive, why wouldn't it surface?

Ophelia lifted her arm to her face and wept.

DDDDD

SHE WAS FIGHTING THE SLIPPAGE of time.

For most of her adult years—the years of enduring, of subsisting, surviving—Ophelia had cut time into segments to speed its passage. This rendered pain peripheral and pulled her attention toward successive horizons of provisional relief. But now that she loved her life, she turned her head from side to side, trying to arrest seconds, feel everything, observe it all, and catch and preserve that which held her before it left her. The more she struggled, the more the pace quickened.

A Great Game commenced on the South Side. Ferin and Angel were judges in this mysterious event, and many other Hollywoodites were participants. On the day before it all began, Stan and Ferin opened their apartment to friends coming in from out of town to try their luck at the Game. Ophelia and Clyde brought up spare sleeping bags and hung out in the kitchen while Ferin went up to the roof to chuck eggs at a car that wouldn't stop honking its horn at nothing. The guests were tired from long car/train/bus rides. They drank coffee and beer and ate thawed waffles, then went out to the lake to spin in circles before launching themselves at each other in clumsy, dizzy embraces.

"Sit and spin and run and hug," Colm called it.

"Spit and shit and spun and hung," amended Stan.

Clyde shrugged.

Aw shucks.

The air turned warm and sweaty.

Business picked up a bit at the Lasik Clinic, but they weren't going to ever offer Ophelia a full-time position. Part-time? Maybe. Maybe. They liked her, although she sometimes spoke softly, so patients had difficulty hearing.

She got home, sad feeling, change in the air though it hadn't manifested yet, and watched the My So-Called Life DVDs that someone had schlepped over from this apartment or that.

"We need air-conditioning in here," said Clyde.

"Why?" snapped Ophelia. "If we're leaving in a couple months, why would we need it?"

"Maybe you're right." Clyde scratched her chin. "I mean, what if we went somewhere you don't need air-conditioning?"

And Ophelia wished she had kept her damn mouth shut.

ﭝﭝﭝﭝﭝ

SPRING TURNED TOWARD SUMMER.

Ophelia branched out with yearning. She took long

walks. She took hundreds of pictures with the tiny camera on her flip phone. She explored all the blocks surrounding her apartment. She ranged across Edgewater, Edgewater Glen, Magnolia Glen, Andersonville, and Lakewood-Balmoral. She went out to clubs playing the blues: B.L.U.E.S., the Hot House, Rosa's, and the Checkerboard. She went down to the beach, closed her eyes, and felt the breeze on her face. She listened for the churning of a surfacing shark, but all she heard were the waves. Nothing fetid on the air. Nothing decaying except the tiny shells and seaweed. A fresh, bracing wind, a humid wind promising storms.

And there were storms. And there were parties. Not Hollywood Parties. Saying goodbye parties. Olivia had let her lease expire and was, in fact, planning a return to London in the fall. Matt was leaving, too, back home to Milwaukee. Ferin had gotten into grad school in New Orleans, so he and Angel had scheduled a trip to that city to sign their lease just off the banks of Lake Pontchartrain. Clyde hadn't said anything certain yet, but Ophelia knew she was looking. Soon, the big building would be full of strangers again.

ꙮꙮꙮ

CLYDE WAS TRUE TO HER word. As soon as the water had slightly warmed (which only happened after Memorial Day), she donned her swimsuit and led Ophelia down to the beach to learn how to swim. At first, it seemed almost a game, and they spent more time laughing at Ophelia's ungainliness, her awkwardness in the water, a contrast to her graceful, dancelike motion on land. Ophelia's hands and feet felt like great clubs that splashed and sank. Clyde shrieked in delight when this happened, and she submerged, swimming in circles around her girlfriend, reaching out to tickle or tug at an arm or a leg.

Floating made the lessons feel real. Swimming seemed to Ophelia like doing many unrelated things at once, but floating was doing only one thing—breathing—and doing it well. The first dozen times she tried, she sank and saw the hazy blue sky recede beneath the rush of water over her eyes. But gradually, she learned to control her buoyancy. She learned to stay afloat: a tugboat, a barge, a raft at sea, or a breaching shark.

Ophelia twisted onto her belly, held her breath, and submerged. The water was green and gold from below, onrushing waves receding into a hazy distance. An obscurity. If there was anything out there, she couldn't see it.

Clyde moved on to the backstroke since the floating had gone so well. "It's like floating, only you're going places. I'll do the backstroke for hours; I'll do it all the way to Michigan; it's just rough if the sun's in your eyes."

For a month, Ophelia and Clyde went to the beach almost daily. Ophelia learned the crawl, the breaststroke, and the sidestroke. She learned to hold her breath for half a minute. She could float on her back and her stomach. She wasn't afraid of the lake anymore. She had tasted its water and dove and surfaced, holding fistfuls of sand.

One night, when the sun had sunk behind the high-rises, leaving the sky the colors of sherbet, that delicious shade of magenta that seems to bleed and begs to be tasted,

Ophelia went out as far as her feet could touch the bottom. She stood on her toes, facing the shore, and the apartment blocks climbed into the air, and the City, in all its immensity, was right there, right in front of her. Ophelia's big toe, the only part of her body touching the earth, was her tether to that world. The rest of her belonged to the lake.

She turned around and looked at the placid water receding all the way to the horizon. Her bobbing head was the only feature disturbing the smooth plane of the lake. She looked for her shark. She saw nothing.

"You're out there," she said. "I'll see you again someday."

ﾊﾊﾊﾊﾊ

AND FLEET TIME FLITED. Now, the solstice had passed, and the shadows, startled into the corners by the endless beating sun, began to creep longer again. Now Clyde bought used Lonely Planet and Rough Guide books and left them lying around the apartment. Voicemails started to add up on Ophelia's phone. Her grandmother. Calling about her dad. Calling about her brother. Who was going to die, and who was going to live, and when, and in what order?

"Tonight, I want to take the train downtown," she told Clyde one evening. "I want to get wasted, walk all the way back along Clark Street, and watch the sunrise over Hollywood with you. Then I want to drink coffee, and eat waffles, and fall into bed with you, and mess around, and then sleep all day long tomorrow."

"Cool," said Clyde. "I want to go see Revenge of the Sith. Think we can do that too?"

THE SUN WAS STILL EVERYWHERE on a workless weekday when Ophelia walked down to Eugene's in Uptown, on a block where the back alley was Edgewater clean, and the front lawn was littered with paper like the ghetto in Rockville. She walked up the three flights of stairs to meet him in his overheated apartment, where flies lazily alighted on dozens of unread books. They drank a dozen beers between them and bitched about Grand Funk and the Stones' Satanic Majesties phase until Eugene's girlfriend made some crack about American-made cars, and then it was knives out.

"They don't got unions like we do over there," Ophelia spat. "They got social clubs of company 'yes men!'"

Her dad would have been proud. Her brother wouldn't have cared.

Then they watched Cowboy Bebop and drank more beers.

Ophelia chose the lake on the walk back, and the summer blue waves crashed crescently against the break walls. Unlike a true ocean, this water never touched the tropics. The approach of winter always notched summer promises. Still, dragonflies wheeled overhead, and the clouds were painted the ruddy undertones of monsoon deluges. The City felt exotic that day, not because of the space that separated it from Rockville but because the City was always receiving outsiders from much farther than that and ejecting its people farther still.

When Ophelia made it back home, she was thoroughly drunk and sloughed up the stairs. She vomited gracefully into the toilet and then moped out to the kitchen to sip some water and stare out the window some more. The windows were open, but the air was torpid and still. When Clyde got home, she warmed some black beans, put Ophelia's feet in her lap, and helped her girlfriend remove her sweaty socks.

"I fought with Eugene's girlfriend today," slurred Ophelia.

"I've thought it over," said Clyde. "When our lease is up, I want to move to Portland. A friend told me she can get me a job at OSHU. Do you want to come with?"

Ophelia puked.

〉〉〉〉〉〉

AFTER THE FOURTH OF JULY, the sooty remnants of spent rockets washed up on the Hollywood beach, and Clyde flew out to Portland to find a sublet.

Ophelia stayed behind, tying up loose ends at the hospital. The Lasik center had decided to convert her temp position into a part-time listing. They offered Ophelia the job, but she couldn't accept it. She was moving to Portland (*right?*), so she recommended Eugene for the job and spent the week training him on the filing system she had built from the ground up. She never felt she'd earned her $10.60 an hour as much as that week.

Clyde called every night, full of rumors and reports.

"I'll be honest," she gushed. "I was worried that we'd end up homeless, so I signed on the first place we saw. It's kinda a one-bedroom and kinda of a studio. It's nice, though. It's just they put some folding doors up over a big closet and called it a one-bedroom. It's really not. But whatever. It's not that expensive. In San Francisco, it's a lot more expensive, right? The woman painted this enormous vulva on the wall. She's a psycho-feminist, the best kind. She said she'd paint over it, but I don't know. I'd kind of like to keep it. What do you think?"

A grainy, pixilated photo followed.

Ophelia chuckled and texted back: *watever u like*

She was excited about Clyde's excitement. She was worried that she wasn't excited about the move herself.

Time flies when you're having fun, she thought. If that doesn't prove that God's cruel, then nothing does.

Brendan and Aley came over, and a couple other Hollywood hangers-on and they went up to Ferin's apartment and watched him plow through a performance art piece that involved a dozen shots of tequila. After every shot, he told a story.

I could hold my liquor better than he does, Ophelia thought.

"How's your ... apartment search ... coming?" asked a very drunk Ferin.

"It's over," said Brendan. "We signed the lease. Stan and Aley and me. We got a place in the Ukrainian Village. We're moving in next month, right after you take off."

"We need to throw that last ... party," gasped Ferin, and he hurried off to the bathroom.

꒰꒰꒰꒰꒰

CLYDE RETURNED THAT WEEKEND, HOLDING the ink-streaked check stub for the deposit on the sublet. She was flush with triumph.

Ophelia wasn't there. Ophelia was back in Rockville. He'd had a fall. She took the train home to cook meals and offer rides to the hospital. To do dishes and laundry, and mop the floors where something sticky had spilled. It was a long weekend. She was ready for the train to take her home. Before leaving, she took a walk in the rain through the hills and furrows of South Village and Ashburn Heights. The inky river slowly churning through. No sharks here, but it was lovely and firefly-full, and it reminded her of a time when this place didn't exhaust her. But still, she dreamed of the City. Now, she had less than a month left on her lease and knew Clyde wouldn't stay an extra day. Clyde was ready to move on. Everyone was.

ノノノノノ

THE FINAL DAYS ARRIVED. THE Hollywood Crew converged upon the old apartment building for Angel's bachelorette party, Ferin's bachelor party, and the long drive to Ohio for the wedding. They were gone for a week afterward. Down to Mexico or Belize or Florida or somesuch for their honeymoon. Stan started moving his stuff out. The banks of computers. The sketches he'd made of peaches and skulls. The furniture he'd scavenged from the alleys. Olivia left for London. Colm and Eliza left for New York. The crew gathered on the beach for every farewell, bathed in beer and music and manifestoes and long shadows, lighter fluid in the air, someone grilling burgers and brats, and who knows what sharks lurked just out of sight. Each time, on the walk home, Clyde grabbed a box from the alley and filled it with books and clothes. The end was coming. It had almost arrived.

꘏꘏꘏꘏꘏

ONE AUGUST AFTERNOON, OPHELIA RETURNED home with a sack full of groceries and heard her phone ringing on the nightstand. She dropped the bag, hurried into her bedroom, and picked it up.

"He's dead!" her grandma said. "They found him in his bed this morning."

This, then, was the event Ophelia had been expecting, quietly, for months now. The moment she'd rehearsed on imagined unlit stages while Clyde snored blissfully beside her. Keep your face straight, Ophelia thought. It's a call about getting change at the laundromat. It's a call about opening a new bank account. It's a call about the stars. Just keep yourself still and let the waves roll past you, like Clyde said.

"I'm sorry," Ophelia said. "How are you?"

"I'm all broken up, inside and outside. I knew this was coming. I knew this was coming. I just didn't know who was going to go first. I guess it was you, you leaving us last year; I was happy to see you getting out. I didn't know how much I'd miss you!"

Ophelia had crossed to the kitchen, taking it in, picking up a pen and a pad, her mouth straight, scratching the tip upon the paper to get the ink flowing.

"When's the funeral?"

"It's at that place on Intervale. They asked if we wanted one room or two. We said one. He didn't know that many people anymore, and I'm not even sure how many of them are going to come. But I feel selfish because maybe … maybe I would have gotten two rooms if I really cared. Just in case everyone shows up!"

"One room is good," said Ophelia. "He wouldn't have wanted you going broke at the funeral. How are you, besides? Are you eating? Drinking?"

"I haven't had an appetite today, but Ross came over and brought me some mac and cheese and mashed potatoes from Bob Evan's."

"Eat those. You need to take care of yourself. You need your energy up because the next few days are gonna take a lot out of you."

"I loved him, Ophelia. He was just broken, but I loved him with all my heart."

I was broken once, Ophelia thought.

"I know," she said.

The door opened and shut. Clyde was coming inside, unshouldering her backpack, watching Ophelia with curiosity.

"I need you," Ophelia's grandma said. "I can't do this on my own. I need you here. I need someone to help with the things I need."

"I know," Ophelia said. "I'm coming. Just as soon as I can."

"Tonight?"

"Tomorrow. I don't have a car, but I'll get a train ticket."

Clyde's eyebrows rose in alarm.

"Get some sleep," Ophelia said.

A few minutes later, she hung up the phone.

"What was that?" Clyde asked.

"My grandma," Ophelia said. "He died."

Clyde breathed in slowly. Out slowly. Ophelia watched her.

"I'm sorry, babe," she said. "How can I help?"

"I've got to go back," said Ophelia.

"When's the funeral?"

"Monday."

A thought had been growing in Ophelia's mind ever since she had picked up the phone. Facts and actions had shouldered aside doubt and dread. I need to do something, thought Ophelia. I know what I need to do.

"My grandma needs my help," she said. "I'm the only one who can help her."

Silence filled the room.

"Do you want me to come with you?" Clyde finally asked.

"No, you have to get ready for your move."

Clyde cocked her head. "Our move."

Ophelia shook her head. "I'm not just going back for the funeral. I'm going back to help my grandma. My grandpa. They've had a hard time managing things on their own, and it's going to be harder now. There's one less person to take care of them. And there's one less person that they love in the world."

"But this is our life!"

"It has been," said Ophelia. "For a whole year. Now, do you know why I just wanted everyone to stay? I couldn't ask that. Of course, I couldn't ask that. But I knew that all this good in my life couldn't last forever. It was impossible. Maybe I was the only one who realized that."

"But I still don't understand. How long? I mean, how long do you think you're going to stay?"

"I don't know."

"I mean, what if I got a sublet? Didn't sign a lease. If you gave me, if you gave me, what, a month, a number of months, I'd just list it on Craigslist, easy as that, just to pay the bills, you know, and then when you were ready, you could fly on out!"

"I don't know how long I'm going to be, Clyde. Maybe weeks. Maybe months. Maybe .... But I don't know. But I don't think you should wait for me. I don't think I'm ready for Portland. I don't think I'm ready to just keep going out, farther and farther, not yet ...."

"Then ... what if I came back with you? I haven't started up at OSHU yet. Are there hospitals in Rockville? There have to be!"

"No," Ophelia said. "I mean, there are, but ... I don't want you to make this journey with me. This time I need to go on my own."

"You sure as hell sound like you've made your mind up!"

Now, Clyde was crying.

"I'm not breaking up with you," Ophelia said.

"You're not not breaking up with me," said Clyde. "I'm going out to the Pacific Ocean! And you're going back to ... that place. Do you really think we'll stay together after this?"

"I want to," said Ophelia. "My God, I want to. I love you. And I don't know how this ends for us. Or for me.

Maybe it ends wonderfully, with us together again! We can hope for that, can't we? I know what you want to do, and I know what I need to do. What you need to do. You need to move out West and take that job at OSHU. I need to go back to Rockville and help my family. But I don't think this is an end. I don't think this is forever."

It's funny. I've dreaded this moment. All year, I've dreamed of this moment and feared it. My fear was so big it kept me awake at night, shaking. But now that it's here, and I know what I need to do, I'm not afraid.

It was a windless afternoon. On Hollywood Beach, two blocks away, the waves came in quietly, in a regular cadence, and the lake was deep and still. The sun beamed from behind a thin screen of clouds.

"You're not leaving now, are you?" sniffed Clyde.

"Tomorrow morning."

"Then you can at least come to the party before you go."

"What party?"

"Don't you remember? There's one more Hollywood party. It's happening on the South Side tonight. It's the last time we're going to be together before everyone leaves. And you too, I guess."

"It's tonight?"

"They're calling it Hospital Happening. We're all supposed to dress up like nurses and doctors and whatever. They're bringing in some nerd rappers or something."

Ophelia smiled.

Violent answered her door with a toothbrush sticking out of her mouth.

"Crmmph erm ern," she said, waving her arms, and they went inside and donned some baggy scavenged scrubs while Violentina traded toothpaste for mouthwash.

Now, they were sitting, all three of them, side-by-side on the Red Line as the train plunged beneath the boughs of the trees, the brick six-flats on shady cul-de-sacs, and underground. Ophelia felt for Clyde's hand. Found it. Held it. No words. Sweat gathered on their clasped palms. Ophelia answered the sweat with a tight squeeze, and Clyde squeezed back so hard it almost hurt. Ophelia liked the pressure. When she glanced at her girlfriend, Clyde's eyes were glassy like a mirror, and Ophelia wondered if these were tears withheld.

Meanwhile, Violent talked about Grace Jones and Grace Slick and how the name "Grace" was an accurate totem of underappreciated genius. Ophelia laughed, and there were tears in her voice, surprise now, and Violent looked at them, puzzled.

Clyde put her hands in her pockets. Aw shucks. Ophelia tried hard not to cry.

Now, the train was above ground again, flanked by the innumerable rough lanes of the Dan Ryan charging north and south.

Now, they were climbing off the train at the platform at Garfield.

Now they were waiting for the languishing buses, and wouldn't you know it?, the buses arrived early this night!

Now the bus was rushing them across the South Side,

into Hyde Park, compressing the night, compressing time, racing them to their destination so they could hurry along to the morning and all that it would bring.

They buzzed the buzzer, and Colm met them in the vestibule. This apartment belonged to the Mysterious Wizards, a South Side arts collective ready to adopt the orphaned children of the Hollywood Group. As Hollywood started to dissolve into memory, these wizards strode their ranks, recruiting, consolidating, communing, ascending with their own music and manifestoes and installations and bowls of plastic bag popcorn.

Ashley met her friends at the door and chided them for not coming sooner to help set up for the party. The setup for this last of the Hollywood parties had been elaborate. There were syringes filled with vodka and Hawai'ian punch. Yes, really. Nobody had skimped on a costume. Everyone wore scrubs, blue or white or gray, or pattered with teddy bears and sunflowers. The Mysterious Wizards had elevated their party game beyond what had been possible at Stan and Ferin's carpeted apartment. They had raised, upon the hardwood floors, a small stage, and right now, Straight Auggie Compte strutted and flung forth slings and cyphers.

Ophelia plucked up a syringe and squeezed breathless spirits down her throat.

The next hours were precious. Genuine witness. The nights were lengthening but not yet long. Not yet cold. Out into the dew for another round of stand-and-spin-and-run-and-hug. Black waves crashed upon the break wall. You got a year, Ophelia thought. Four percent of your life has been here. The past is closed. A door slams shut. But look up. There is no ceiling. The night is open. It was hard not to see this gorgeous night, this terrible night, glamor-infused, magic eluding the eyes but running the veins, more potent than any drug Ophelia's brother or father ever tasted, as an end to all things wonderful. It was hard to imagine that what followed could possibly be wonderful and nourishing, or even good and tolerable when she was heading back to Rockville to care for sick and sad people while Clyde moved on to the brink of forests and volcanoes and unbearable oceans. But after all that this year, the Hollywood Group, Clyde, and her shark had given her, Ophelia felt able to say:

"Wake up, wake up, you only get this day, today, once!"

Two am ticked by, and three am, and four. SAC finished his set. The syringes had been thoroughly drained. Now, the girls strode through the apartment, tired in their bras, while boys nodded on slack couches, wakeful enough, and persistent recruiters among the Mysterious Wizards lobbied the last of the orphans to sign leases and help take over the building. Now, the faint traces of light in the sky—western glow, eastern promise, an ever-present haze of green-yellow sulfur vying with the stars for the mastery of heaven— danced and fought. Now, the night was endless. Now, the night was not endless. Now, Ophelia spoke to anyone who would listen and listened to anyone who could speak.

"The pop-not-soda thing doesn't apply to Milwaukee," said Matt. "We call it soda. We call it what we want."

"Next stop, Thailand," said Pearl.

"The thing about beaches is you don't have to take care of them," said Gray. "They take care of themselves as long as you're barefoot."

"The problem with the Great Game," said Angel, "is that they don't want to change the Great Game. But everything that lasts changes. Nothing stays the same forever. You must be ready to change if you want to stick around."

"Um," said Colm. "Ummmmmmm." And he scratched his messy head.

"I will never forget this," said Ashley. "Even if I live another ten years!"

"In one week," said Ferin, "I'll be on Bourbon Street, drinking cafe au lait and eating, you know, those donut thingies. Shoot me your address in Rockville. I'll mail them to you. I'll honestly just send you a whole box full. I can't wait to drive across that big lake."

"He kept talking about China," said Chris.

"I kept talking about China," said Stan. "I don't know. I want to build something, you know? I want to buy the parts and make it from scratch. It doesn't have to last forever. It just has to be fun while it lasts. I want to see the Northern Lights. I almost got to last year, but the City was too bright, and I couldn't get out far enough. I couldn't get to where I could see the sky clearly."

"We're off to New York," said Eliza. "We're going to beat a drum and watch all the Spike Lee movies that take place when it's hot out. You know that, right? Spike Lee movies that take place in the winter all suck, but the ones filmed in the heat all rock your socks off."

"On my thirtieth birthday, I want corned beef and cabbage and Guinness and Bushmills at a real Irish Pub," said Brendan. "That's a few years away, so I've got time to plan!"

Or something like that.

The East was slowly becoming brighter than the West.

"I'll wait for you, you know," said Clyde.

"I don't hate you if you don't," said Ophelia.

"No," said Clyde. "But you know what I'm going to do first thing when I arrive in Portland? I'm going to buy a little cactus and put it on the windowsill, water it once a week, and keep it alive for years and years. And no matter what happens—if you come or if you don't—I'll keep it alive and look after it, and every time I look at it, I'll think of you. You're right. This year has been something else. I wouldn't be me today if I wasn't with you yesterday."

"My train will be leaving in a few hours," Ophelia said. "I think I have to head back to the apartment one last time."

"You want to catch a nap first? I don't blame you … knowing what you're heading back to."

"No," said Ophelia. "There's someone I need to say goodbye to. For the last time. Not you. Because I know I'm going to see you again. But there's someone else. Someone I'm never going to see again."

〰〰〰〰〰〰

THE SKY WAS BRIGHT, THE sun perched just beneath the horizon, when Ophelia returned to Hollywood Beach, swimsuit-clad, shivering in the slightest chill of oncoming autumn. Nobody there, all alone, as she had always been alone whenever she had seen her friend.

Her living friend.

Her hidden friend.

Now, Ophelia knew how to swim.

Far to the West: Portland.

Not so far to the East: Rockville.

Here, now: the City.

And the lake.

Out there: a monster, a voice, a possibility.

Ophelia went into the water.

She went out where her toes couldn't touch the sandy bottom.

She wasn't afraid. She was full of life and hope. Her legs were strong because she had walked many miles and because Clyde had taught her how to swim. Her arms were powerful, and they waked the waves behind her. Long strides that drew her far out, away from the shore and the reassuring sand.

Ophelia swam toward the dawn.

She wasn't afraid.

She was swimming from one end into a new beginning.

She knew the shark was out there, alive, waiting, listening, looking.

She wanted to thank it. To bless it. To kiss it. To show some grace in exchange for the grace she had received.

Ophelia wasn't afraid.

She was ready.